RAFE'S ISLAND

GINA WILKINS

From The Library Of
BARBARA L. OLSON

Harlequin Books

TORONTO • NEW YORK • LONDON
AMSTERDAM • PARIS • SYDNEY • HAMBURG
STOCKHOLM • ATHENS • TOKYO • MILAN
MADRID • WARSAW • BUDAPEST • AUCKLAND

For Sue Easterby and Teri Sanders—my sight-seeing buddies and moral support team from St. Louis. You're very special friends.

Published September 1993

ISBN 0-373-25558-6

RAFE'S ISLAND

Prologue

RAFE DANCER turned up the cuffs of his fine white cotton shirt, then brushed absently at a speck of dust on his crisp white slacks. He stood on a bluff overlooking a tropical paradise of sandy beaches and brilliantly colored flowers, an island resort of clever little cottages, swimming pools, tennis courts and riding trails. White Jeeps darted cheerfully from the main resort to the north landing, where regularly scheduled launches carried scantily clad tourists to the larger islands nearby for shopping and sight-seeing. Serendipity was a utopia of light and color, a refuge from the harsh realities of the outside world.

And yet Rafe felt as though a pall lay over the resort, which dimmed the brilliance of the sun and muted the gaiety of the colors. As though the shadows inside him were seeping out to surround him, despite his relentless efforts to keep them locked away.

On his good days, he could forget the past, push back the memories, allow himself to enjoy the resort he'd worked so hard to build. He could take pride in creating this refuge that, through his own ingenuity and careful planning, had grown increasingly profitable.

On the bad days, the memories clawed their way back up from the darkest depths of his mind to torment him with images of death, deceit and betrayal. At those times, the people closest to him knew to stay away, to give him room and time to push those mental doors closed again.

This wasn't one of his good days.

And so, he was rather surprised that his solitude in this place that was generally regarded as his private retreat was abruptly interrupted.

"Um—Mr. Dancer?"

Rafe turned to find one of his resort employees only a few feet away, looking at him with questioning brown eyes. It was a measure of his deeply introspective mood that the young man had managed to come so close without Rafe's hearing him. There'd been a time when such carelessness on his part would have gotten him killed.

"What is it, Joe?"

Joe cleared his throat and watched his boss rather warily as he extended a slip of paper. "It's a telegram, sir. Jeanette thought you might want to see it immediately, so she asked me to find you."

Expecting bad news, Rafe sighed and took the note, which was written in his secretary's meticulous script:

Courtney Elise Parrish was born yesterday, weighing in at seven and a half pounds. Mother

*and daughter are doing very well. Father still re-
cuperating. Invite you to admire incredibly
beautiful child in person, whenever you can slip
away from paradise.*

Rafe was smiling by the time he reached the end of the
brief message. The smile surprised him almost as
much as it seemed to startle Joe.

"Er—good news, sir?" Joe asked carefully.

"Very good news."

"Oh. That's . . . good. Do you need anything else,
Mr. Dancer?"

"No, that's all. Tell Jeanette she was right about my
wanting to see this now."

"I will."

"Thanks, Joe."

Alone again, Rafe stroked his thumb along the firm
line of his jaw as he thought about the telegram. So his
formerly footloose friend Tristan Parrish was now a
father. Wouldn't that astonish those skeptics who'd
doubted that the restless, daring, commitment-shy,
foreign-correspondent-turned-news-anchor would
ever settle down to domestic life? Rafe would have
been surprised himself had he not met Tristan's wife,
Devon, and recognized the strength of the bonds between the couple. Bonds that had never existed between Rafe and the woman to whom he'd been
married for a very brief time in his youth.

Maybe that was one of his problems, he mused.
He'd made a success of the resort he'd built after leav-

ing his government job, but he was still alone. He could hardly remember the last time he'd even had dinner with a woman, other than for business reasons.

Women tended to be nervous around him, even when they were attracted to him. As though they sensed that his easy smile and casual conversation were only a facade that concealed things they couldn't begin to understand. Things like a potential for violence kept sternly leashed, but always there. Like memories that would make anyone cringe in distaste. Like the old, haunting doubts about whether the success he'd found in his former career had been worth the methods he'd sometimes employed to achieve his ends.

His ex-wife had never learned to accept the darker side of him, had never understood his need to retreat into himself at times. She'd been drawn at first to the excitement of his dangerous job, then eventually repelled and threatened by it. After they'd split up— long before he'd left his former career—he'd avoided serious relationships, doubting that any woman could live with his work.

Even now, his government job long behind him, his current career hardly a threat to anyone, he was still cautious, waiting until he was sure he'd put his past far enough behind him ever to burden anyone else. And though he still wasn't sure he was ready for the sort of ties Tristan had forged with Devon, Rafe privately admitted that he was lonely, that his business success wasn't enough to completely fill that aching void inside him.

Maybe he *would* make a short trip to Atlanta. It would take him a few weeks to clear his schedule, but he should be able to get away by the end of next month. He hadn't seen Tristan and Devon since he'd attended their wedding a year or so earlier. And he'd like very much to see the "incredibly beautiful" Courtney Elise Parrish.

As he made his way down the rocky, flower-lined path leading back to his office, he noted with satisfaction that the imaginary shadows had receded. The sun shone brightly around him, the tropical colors as vivid as ever.

It seemed he had Tristan to thank for dispelling the darkness this time.

1

T. J. HARRIS STEPPED off a curb one Tuesday afternoon in late May and was almost run down by a speeding car. Only her companion's shout of warning and her own quick reflexes saved her from being struck by the dark, deadly vehicle. The car missed her by mere inches and never even slowed as it sped away.

"T.J.!" Gayle Kennedy grabbed her friend's arm, eyes wide with horror. "Are you all right?"

Although frightened, T.J. reacted with characteristic fury as she pushed her shaggy sable bangs out of her eyes and glared after the vehicle, noting that it didn't bear a license plate. "You jerk, you almost killed me!" she shouted. "Damn drunk driver," she muttered with a disgusted shake of her head.

"If you'd been one second slower..." Gayle shuddered. "Oh, T.J., I can't even think about it."

"I'm okay, Gayle. I'm just glad you noticed in time to warn me. The way he came out of nowhere like that, I didn't even see him until he was almost on top of me."

"We should call the police and report that guy," Gayle announced heatedly. "Let's find a phone."

"And tell them what? That a dark car with no license plate nearly turned me into street pizza? It wouldn't do any good, Gayle."

"Ugh." Gayle made a face at her friend. "Honestly, T.J., that's disgusting."

T.J. managed a slightly shaky laugh. "Sorry. Guess I'm still hacked off."

"Understandably so. Do you still feel like going shopping, or would you rather go home?"

T.J. shook her head in fond exasperation. She and Gayle had been friends since high school, but were as different as any two women could possibly be. Though both were the same age—twenty-six—they had chosen very different paths to follow in their lives.

Gayle, the devoted wife of a podiatrist and the proud mother of three, was contentedly domestic, her energies devoted to cleaning and decorating her home and nurturing her family. T.J., on the other hand, was a reporter for an Atlanta newspaper, so consumed by her career that she had very little life away from her work. Her few romantic relationships had self-destructed and the occasional secret longing for a family of her own was overridden by the demands of deadlines and story chasing. Still, T.J. and Gayle had made every effort to maintain their friendship, which had meant so much to both of them over the years.

"Why would I want to abandon our shopping trip just because some drunk got behind the wheel of a car?" T.J. asked logically. "I'm not going to have a fit of the vapors, Gayle."

Gayle laughed and tossed her strawberry-blond hair. "No, of course you're not. I should have known missing death by inches was just routine for a daring, adventurous reporter like the renowned T. J. Harris."

T.J. scowled and stepped off the curb again—after checking very carefully for oncoming traffic. "Yeah, right. Renowned for a series of fluffy feature pieces about prominent Atlanta society leaders. Somehow I doubt I'll be nominated for a Pulitzer for the work I've been doing the past six weeks."

Gayle lingered in front of a store window that displayed a collection of sparkling crystal. "You're lucky to have a job at all," she commented frankly. "I keep warning you that your temper is going to get you fired someday if you don't learn to moderate it with a little tact. You shouldn't have told your editor that he was turning the newspaper into a butt-licking, politician-pandering gossip sheet."

"Well, he is," T.J. grumbled. "I just can't convince him that there's no such thing as 'politically correct' journalism. A good journalist reports the facts, without considering whether they'll be received with public approval. It's like that little newspaper in Arkansas I heard about. The owners and editors gave in to public pressure and completely stopped reporting anything about a serious, local toxic-waste problem because the community leaders thought it made the town look bad and real-estate agents were worried that house prices would plummet. I thought that sort of thing could never happen at my paper, but this hotshot new editor won't let anything past unless it's approved by the editorial staff, the lawyers, the PR people and the advertising department. It's sickening."

"You're still going to have to be less outspoken with your criticism," Gayle argued. "You certainly aren't going to get any promotions where you are unless you learn to compromise. Maybe even give in at times."

"I'd rather sell pencils on a street corner."

"Right. Which is why you're doing a series of society feature articles rather than lose your job."

T.J. winced at the direct hit. "Okay, so I've got bills to pay. But I'm sending out résumés first thing next week. I can't take this much longer."

"You may hate them, but I'm enjoying your articles. You're doing such a great job of showing up the shallow, insincere subjects without ever overtly accusing them of anything. They're probably very flattered by the articles, even though I know you're really making fun of them."

"That's because you know me so well. Actually, some of them are really pretty nice people, who are genuinely committed to the causes they've adopted. But then there are others . . ." She shuddered expressively.

"Like Judy McBain?" Gayle suggested.

"Exactly. What a dip. It's a wonder our esteemed Councilman McBain allows her out in public. Not that he treats her all that well in private. You should have heard the way he talked to her when we accidentally walked in on him and an associate during a tour of their house. I wouldn't talk to a dog that way. I never did like that guy, but I could almost feel sorry for his wife after hearing him snarl at her."

"Which must be why you went relatively easy on her in the article. Of course, you did work in that priceless quote 'If only everyone would treat each other politely and start following the rules, our city would be so much nicer.' Did she *really* say that?"

"With wide-eyed conviction," T.J. replied with a sigh. "I've got to find a new job. Hey, look at the little red dress in that store window. Wouldn't Nick like to see you in that one?"

"In his dreams! That dress is designed for someone six inches taller and twenty pounds lighter than I am."

T.J. absently brushed a hand through her short, shaggy hair. For several years she'd worn it in a chin-length bob, but she'd had it cut recently to a wispy, boyish cap, and it still felt a bit unfamiliar when she ran her fingers through it. "I don't know," she said thoughtfully, picturing her friend in the flirty, sexy garment in the store window. "It might look great. Why don't you try it on?"

"No way. *You* try it on."

"Yeah, right. Like I've got someplace to wear a strapless sequined dress. You're the one with the thriving social life, remember?"

"Haven't I been trying to fix you up with some of Nick's friends? If you'd only go out with one of them instead of wasting your free time hanging out in that tacky bar with your reporter buddies...."

T.J. laughed and linked her arm through Gayle's as they entered into the familiar debate with enthusiasm, the incident with the careless driver already half-forgotten.

RAFE GLANCED at the two men climbing out of the car with him and then at the out-of-the-mainstream bar they planned to enter Wednesday evening. "I'm not at all sure this is safe," he murmured.

Tristan Parrish lifted an inquiring eyebrow beneath the lock of golden-blond hair that tumbled over his forehead in a way so many women seemed to find irresistible—not that it did them any good now that Tristan had found his Devon. "It's not the most upscale bar in Atlanta, but I assure you it's perfectly safe. The clientele tends to be made up of reporters and off-duty cops. I've brought Neal here a couple of times and we've never gotten into trouble yet, have we, Neal?"

Tristan's friend Neal Archer, whom Rafe had met at Tristan's wedding, chuckled. "No. Not at this place, anyway."

"I was remembering the night we met," Rafe explained to Tristan. "After you rescued me from those guerrilla soldiers, we headed for the nearest bar and got disgustingly drunk. Thought I was going to die the next morning—and I almost wanted to."

Tristan laughed and reached for the door handle. "We'll try to restrain ourselves tonight. I'm a respectable married man and father these days. I don't get disgustingly drunk anymore."

"Oh, I remember a time not so long ago when you overindulged in this very bar," Neal murmured, following Tristan and Rafe inside.

Tristan grimaced at Rafe's questioning look. "It's a long story," he muttered.

"I'll have to hear it sometime," Rafe replied with a grin. Still smiling, he glanced around the dimly lighted bar. The familiar scents of booze and tobacco, the sound of jukebox music and muffled voices made him feel immediately at ease. He'd spent a lot of time in shadowy bars, in his own country and a dozen others. And though he'd thought his past well behind him, he was startled by a feeling of nostalgia. Odd.

Tristan glanced at Rafe and sighed. "You used to blend right into the shadows in a place like this. Now you stand out like a neon sign."

Rafe wasn't troubled by Tristan's accusation. He knew his white sweater and slacks were quite visible. He'd had more than enough of blending into shadows. It felt good to know it didn't matter that his light-colored clothing made him a perfect target. No one had a reason to be aiming at him now.

"Hey, Tristan! Over here!"

The jovial yell drew the attention of the three men to a small table in a far corner where a heavyset, bearded man waved a meaty arm. Tristan nodded an acknowledgment. "Mitchell Drisco," he explained to Rafe. "A cameraman from my station. Nice guy. Oh, and that's T. J. Harris with him. A reporter for the local newspaper. You should find T.J. very... interesting."

Rafe wondered at the speculative look Tristan gave him, and at Neal's quiet chuckle. "It's okay with me if you want to join them for a drink," he assured them.

The cameraman stood as Rafe, Tristan and Neal approached. "Yo, Tris. Whatcha doing out tonight?" he demanded with a mocking grin. "Thought you'd be home with the wife and daughter."

"My wife and daughter are hosting a baby shower at our house tonight," Tristan explained. "The guys have been kicked out for a few hours. Neal, you remember Mitchell Drisco and T. J. Harris?"

"Of course." Neal pulled a chair to the undersize table as Mitchell shifted to accommodate them.

Tristan nodded his chin toward Rafe. "This is Rafe Dancer, a friend of mine who owns a resort in the Caribbean—a place I highly recommend if either of you gets an urge for a tropical vacation."

"Don't I wish." Mitchell sighed. "Nice to meet you, Rafe. Grab a chair."

Rafe snagged an empty chair from a nearby table and turned it to the table where Tristan and Neal had already been seated, leaving him to slide in beside T.J. Only when he'd settled into the chair did he glance at the reporter, and found himself being studied by a pair of inquisitive brown eyes. Feminine eyes. For the first time, he realized that T. J. Harris was a woman—and a very attractive one, at that.

She was slouched comfortably in her seat, her long, denim-clad legs stretched in front of her. She was slim and tanned, her skin flawless, her features striking. Her eyes were an unusual golden brown with long, lush dark lashes. Her unpainted mouth was just a shade too wide, the lower lip full and soft. She wore her hair rather shaggy, and very short—even shorter than his own, but he rather fancied the style on this woman. Maybe because the style bared such a nice neck and such delicate ears.

Tristan was right. Rafe thought T. J. Harris very interesting, indeed.

T.J. FOUND HERSELF caught and held by Rafe Dancer's speculative gaze. She'd been fascinated by him from the moment he'd approached the table behind Tristan and Neal, a tall, lean, muscular man whose white clothing contrasted strikingly with his longish, jet black hair and dark, rough-hewn features. His smile was friendly and relaxed, but he'd moved with the lethal grace of a wild animal. Which might explain the shiver of wariness that coursed down her spine when their eyes met.

His eyes . . .

So dark the irises were almost indistinguishable from the pupils, his obsidian eyes gleamed with intelligence and studied her with an unsettling intensity. There were ghosts in those piercing eyes, a darkness that repelled her even as his flashing smile beckoned her.

Mentally shaking off her disturbing impression, she chided herself for being foolish. It had been years since she'd allowed herself to be intimidated by any man, and she had no intention of letting this one do so. She gave him a cool nod of greeting and forced her attention back to Tristan. "So, who's the baby shower for?" she asked, glancing speculatively at Neal, who had married within the past year. "Anyone I know?"

Tristan, too, looked at Neal with a grin. "Oh, yeah. Neal's going to be a father again in a few months. He and Holly found out just last week that they're having twins."

"Twins?" T.J. smiled, taking in Neal's rather dazed expression. "Should I congratulate you or offer condolences?"

Neal sighed and shrugged ruefully. "Holly and I agreed to have one child, after we'd been married a while longer. I should have known she'd get pregnant entirely by accident—and with twins."

"You can hardly blame it all on Holly," Tristan murmured, motioning for a waitress. "I would guess you were involved in this."

"I never said it was all Holly's fault," Neal retorted. "I only meant that I should have known not to try to make plans. Holly's been creating havoc in my once-orderly life ever since we met."

"And you love it," Tristan said.

"I love it," Neal agreed with a contented smile.

Neal's expression gave T.J. a faint, hollow feeling deep inside her. The same sort of feeling she got whenever she noticed how happy Gayle looked when talking about her husband and children. The same way she'd felt on the few occasions when she'd seen Tristan and Devon together, so deeply in love and so smugly pleased with their condition.

It wasn't that she wanted to get married or anything, she assured herself hastily. It was just that she'd like to know how it felt to be that fully committed to another person.

"Are you happy about the babies?" she asked Neal to distract her thoughts.

"Oh, sure. Now that I've had a little time to get used to the idea, I'm really looking forward to them. I've almost forgotten what it's like to have a baby around—my daughter Sara will be twenty-two in a few weeks. At least she and her husband have decided to wait a few years before they start their own family. I'm not sure I could adjust to being a new father and a grandfather all at the same time."

T.J. turned back to Tristan. "Speaking of new fathers . . . how's Courtney?"

Tristan beamed and reached for his pocket. "Perfect," he declared.

Neal and Rafe both groaned.

"Now you've done it," Neal accused T.J. "He's going to bring out the pictures again. All one hundred and seventy of them."

"Six. I have six photos of her," Tristan said, defending himself. "And T.J. and Mitchell really want to see them, don't you?"

T.J. and Mitchell solemnly assured their friend that they were both anxious to see the six photographs of his infant daughter.

The conversation centered on Tristan's family for the next few minutes, then shifted to items of general interest in recent news. Neal, Tristan and Mitchell ordered beers, Rafe coffee. T.J. requested a refill of her diet soft drink, which she sipped while the others talked. She only hoped she was doing an adequate job of concealing her intense awareness of the man at her side.

More than once she felt him watching her, and it was all she could do not to look back at him. She was concerned that if she did, those too-knowing eyes of his would see how strongly he affected her. And when his knee brushed hers beneath the table—accidentally?—she just managed to hide her shiver of reaction.

What was it about Rafe Dancer that was turning her into an awkward adolescent? She couldn't even remember the last time any man had affected her this way. So why this one?

"I read your article in the paper this morning, T.J.," Tristan commented.

His gently mocking tone made her narrow her eyes in warning. "Yes? And did you want to comment on it, Parrish?" she asked, a bit too sweetly.

His expression was all innocence. "I found it quite delightful," he assured her, his British accent stronger than usual. "I've been surprised at how well you've adapted to the society pages. All this time, I've thought your heart was in hard news, when really you were longing to mingle with the beautiful people— Ouch! Dammit, Tyler Jessica, that hurt!"

T.J. drew her booted foot back with a scowl of satisfaction. "One more word about my society pieces and you're going to walk with a permanent limp," she threatened him over the laughter of their friends. "And *don't* call me 'Jessica'!"

"Someday, T.J.," Tristan muttered, rubbing his bruised leg beneath the table. "Someday..."

"Hey, T.J. Maybe it was Tristan driving that car that almost hit you yesterday," Mitchell suggested with a broad grin. T.J. had told him about the near accident, but had downplayed how very close the vehicle had come to hitting her. She knew he wouldn't have teased her about it had he known that she'd missed death by only a matter of inches.

"You were almost hit by a car yesterday?" Rafe asked, his smile fading.

T.J. thought the concern in his deep voice was curious, since he hardly knew her. "Drunk driver," she explained. "I was shopping with a friend and was almost run down. I wasn't hurt or anything, but I was furious."

"Did you report the license number?" Tristan asked, the genuine affection he felt for her obvious in his expression.

She shrugged. "No tags. I looked. Just a big, dark car with no special markings. It would have been a waste of time to report it."

Neal frowned. "That's unusual. You're sure it was just an accident?"

She was surprised by the question. "Of course. Why would you ask that?"

Neal shook his head. "Just being paranoid, I guess. I tend to think reporters are always in personal danger. Comes from having a daredevil friend in the profession, I suppose," he added with a meaningful look at Tristan.

"I gave all that up when I took the desk job," Tristan said without regret. "Nothing dangerous about an anchor spot."

"Nothing dangerous about a series of society pieces, either," T.J. commented, knowing her own regret and frustration must be apparent in her voice. "Damn, but I hate this assignment. I've gotta get out of this job."

"If only you'd learn when to keep your mouth shut," Tristan told her with a resigned exasperation, knowing the full story behind her punitive society assignment.

"Yeah. She'll learn that about the same time pigs learn to fly," Mitchell muttered into his beer, and earned a glare from T.J. "Anybody want anything else to drink?" he asked hastily.

Deciding she needed some fresh air, T.J. reached beneath the table for her soft leather hobo bag. Sitting so close to Rafe Dancer had her nerves thrumming in a way that was as disturbing as it was intriguing. And since she still wasn't quite sure what it was about him that made her react so strongly, she thought she'd do the prudent thing and leave. Before she was tempted to do something foolish, like asking him if he'd like to have dinner with her one evening while he was in town. "I guess I'd better go. I have an early interview in the morning."

"Who is it this time?" Tristan inquired.

She made a face. "Buffy Saint Martin."

Tristan snorted, but wisely refrained from further comment.

"Do you have a car?" Rafe asked, watching as T.J. threw some bills on the table to cover her drinks.

She glanced quickly at him, then away. "I'm parked down the street."

Rafe stood when she did. "I'll walk with you."

Startled, she looked up at him. At five-seven, she wasn't accustomed to having a man tower over her. He must stand a good four inches over six feet. "Thank you, but that's not necessary. This is a pretty safe neighborhood."

"It's never safe for a woman to be alone on the streets after dark," Rafe corrected her. "I'll walk you."

Mitchell gulped loudly. "Careful, Rafe."

"Um— Rafe—" Tristan murmured in warning.

T.J. stopped in front of her battered little economy car and shoved her key in the driver's door. "I guess I'll thank you for the unnecessary escort."

He smiled. "Very gracious. You're welcome, anyway."

Gripping the door handle, she looked pointedly at his hand, which still rested on her arm. "Um—good night, Rafe. Nice meeting you."

"I'd like to see you again. Will you have dinner with me while I'm in town?"

She hesitated for a long moment, torn between her better judgment and the inexplicable temptation to spend more time with Rafe. She tried to think logically, like the experienced professional woman she was rather than some overwhelmed ingenue.

Okay, so she was attracted to him. Who wouldn't be? He was great looking, sexy, virile. Somehow different from most of the men she knew. And what if she was intensely curious about him? Big deal. She'd bet her press card he'd have some riveting stories to tell should she delve into his past. Any dedicated journalist would be fascinated by this man.

She wasn't interested in a one-night stand with a man who was just passing through town, had never gone in for that sort of casual encounter. And something about the gleam in Rafe's eyes made her doubt that he had an evening of innocuous conversation in mind for them. The sensible thing to do, of course, was to politely but firmly turn down his invitation. She opened her mouth to do just that.

"All right. When?" she heard herself saying, instead. And then gulped in astonishment. Why had she said *that*?

Rafe smiled with faint satisfaction. "Tomorrow evening? I've rented a car. Shall I pick you up at seven?"

What the hell. Time to prove—to both of them—that he didn't intimidate her in the least. She'd let him buy her dinner and then she'd send him back to his island and put him completely out of her mind. "All right. Seven. Tristan can give you directions to my place."

"Fine. I'll look forward to it."

Still, his hand lingered on her arm until she cleared her throat and shifted her weight. "Was there anything else?" she asked.

"Just this," he murmured.

And covered her mouth with his.

The kiss was a brief one. Nothing more than a press of lips. Yet T.J. was clinging to her car when it ended, her knees having turned to cream cheese. She couldn't even imagine what it would be like to have him *really* kiss her.

Rafe gave her a self-satisfied smile. "Nice to have that out of the way this quickly, isn't it?" he murmured. "Good night, T.J. Drive carefully."

Only then did he release her arm and step back.

T.J. threw open her car door and climbed quickly behind the wheel and drove away as quickly as the law allowed. She didn't take a full breath until she'd left Rafe Dancer far behind.

She really shouldn't have agreed to go out with him, she told herself dazedly. Any other man would have found himself sprawled on the sidewalk after pulling a stunt like that with her! But there was something about Rafe Dancer that made her act completely unlike herself. And she didn't like feeling that much out of control. Didn't like it at all.

2

RAFE WAS BEMUSED when Tristan, Neal and Mitchell broke into applause as he slid back into his chair. "What's this for?" he asked.

"That's the first time we've ever seen T.J. lose a battle of wills," Tristan explained. He looked at Neal. "Didn't I tell you it would take a man with nerves of steel to handle her?"

Neal smiled. "As I recall, you referred to another part of the male anatomy."

Tristan shrugged and turned back to Rafe. "So, what did you think of her?"

"I'm taking her to dinner tomorrow night."

"You asked her out?" Mitchell's jaw dropped. "And she agreed?"

"Yeah." Rafe nodded acceptance when the waitress offered to freshen his coffee. "Why not?"

"Hell, I don't know. I just can't remember the last time T.J. had a date. She swore off men after she stopped seeing Paul Davis last year. Said she was giving up on trying to tailor her life to suit anyone else. She wasn't in love with the guy or anything, but she said it frustrated her that she couldn't seem to manage even a casual relationship. That stubborn streak and her temper always get in the way."

"Her temper doesn't concern me," Rafe remarked.

"And when it comes to stubborn, Rafe can match her any day," Tristan added. "This might prove to be a very interesting match."

Rafe frowned. "I'm only taking her to dinner, Tristan."

"Mmm. That's what I thought the first time I took Devon out."

"And I only went out with Holly to discuss a photo assignment I wanted her to do for my company," Neal said, smiling at Rafe's wary expression.

Mitchell snorted. "Disgusting, isn't it?" he asked Rafe. "These guys used to be dedicated bachelors. Now not only are they tied and shackled, they're trying to rope all their buddies into the same predicament." He shoved his chair back noisily. "Think I'll get out of here while my single status is intact."

"Don't worry, Drisco. It would take a real whiz of a matchmaker to come up with a mate for you," Tristan retorted.

Mitchell's grin gleamed from behind his bushy beard. "Ain't it the truth. See you guys around."

"Think it's safe to go home now?" Tristan asked, glancing at his watch.

Neal nodded cautiously. "Surely the shower guests are gone by now. How long can it take to open some baby gifts and eat those fancy little cakes?"

"You'd be surprised," Tristan answered with a groan. "Still, I think we should go. Gotta get Rafe in bed early. The man needs his rest if he's going out with T.J. tomorrow. He's going to need his wits about him. Clear thinking, quick reflexes—that's what it'll take if this date's going to be a success."

Rafe rose, shaking his head in exasperation at Tristan's teasing. "You make her sound like the dragon woman. Trust me. I can handle her."

"Famous last words," his friend muttered, limping noticeably from T.J.'s well aimed kick as they headed for the door.

AS THE MEN HOPED, the baby shower had ended by the time they arrived back at Tristan's house. Only Devon, Holly and Neal's daughter Sara remained. Sara cooed over little Courtney while Devon and Holly packed up the many baby gifts Holly had received that evening.

Rafe watched from the background as Tristan and Neal greeted their wives and daughters lovingly. He wondered what it would be like to have someone waiting on Serendipity to greet him as warmly when he returned from his vacation.

He told himself it must be all this talk of marriage and babies making him so uncharacteristically sentimental this evening. He liked his independence, being able to leave home for a couple of weeks without consulting anyone, being free to ask out an attractive woman he'd just met. It would take a very special woman to make him want to trade that freedom for the major responsibilities of marriage and children.

"And here we thought you guys were out having a wild night on the town," Holly Archer said with a laugh, crossing her arms over her enlarged stomach. "You're not even inebriated."

"One beer," Neal replied with a smile. "This is about as wild as it gets for me, sweet pea."

She laughed at him. "I thought I'd taught you how to have fun, sailor."

"Mmm," he murmured. "Why don't we go home and you can give me a refresher course?"

"There they go again," Sara said with a gusty sigh, smiling at Rafe as she spoke. "They're like a couple of infatuated school kids. And I think it's great."

She turned her attention to the others. "I'd better go. Phillip will be wondering what's keeping me. Good night, everyone."

She kissed her father, then her young stepmother. "Take care of my little brothers and/or sisters," she remarked cheerily.

"I'll walk you to your car," Rafe offered. "I think I'll head back to my hotel and turn in early."

Rafe accepted an invitation to have breakfast with Devon and Tristan and bade the others good-night before walking outside with Sara.

"Thanks for the escort," Sara said at the door of her car. "I like a man with nice manners," she added artlessly.

Rafe smiled wryly, thinking of T.J.'s very different reaction to his courteous gesture. He was already anticipating spending more time with the lovely, spirited reporter, despite her friends' teasing about her temper. Meek, submissive women had never appealed to him.

T. J. Harris, on the other hand, appealed to him very much.

BY THE TIME seven o'clock rolled around Thursday evening, T.J. had convinced herself that she had totally overreacted to Rafe Dancer the night before. Maybe she'd just been tired from a long, unsatisfying day at work. He was just another man, interesting but hardly unique. One date, and he'd go back to his island.

She could handle that.

And then her heart leaped right into her throat when her doorbell rang, shattering her carefully constructed excuses. T.J. took several deep breaths before answering the door, scolding herself the entire time for acting like an utter fool.

He was wearing white again, this time a beautifully tailored, loosely fitting suit with a white shirt and tie. There wasn't a smudge, a crease or a fleck of lint anywhere on him. Not a jet black hair out of place, though he wore it long enough to brush his crisply pressed collar. His tie hung perfectly straight, and a white handkerchief stood sharply at attention inside his breast pocket.

T.J. resisted the urge to reach up and smooth her hair or check to make sure nothing was out of place anywhere else on her body. Even dressed in her best silk dress, she felt somewhat disheveled next to this fashionably dressed man. And she wasn't the type of woman who usually worried about what she was wearing.

"Hello, T.J."

His deep voice was a bit husky when he said her name, like smooth whiskey laced with gravel. Had she not been so cautious about romantic entanglements, she suspected that she would have been fighting an urge to hear him murmur her name again—in a more intimate circumstance.

She cleared her throat forcefully. "Hi, Rafe. I hope you didn't have any trouble finding my apartment."

"No trouble at all." He glanced around the functionally furnished room, in which she spent only a minimum amount of time between working hours. "Have you lived here long?"

Knowing he'd noticed the lack of personal touches, she shrugged. "Eighteen months or so. I'm not home much."

"I see." His gaze turned back to her.

She thought about offering him a drink, then promptly rejected the idea. The sooner they were out in public, the better, as far as she was concerned. "I'll get my purse."

The car he'd rented was designed more for performance than style. She wondered what sort of vehicle he'd choose for himself—something this functional or a sleek, powerful sports car? For some reason, the latter seemed more suited to him.

With what she was beginning to accept as characteristic courtesy, Rafe held her door until she had settled into the vehicle, then closed it for her before rounding the front of the car to slide behind the wheel. Again she noted the grace with which he moved. He was sexy, rather elegant and yet unquestionably male, she mused, trying to find words to describe this unusual man.

The latch of her seat belt was stubborn and she muttered curses before it finally clicked. She heard a sound that could have been a chuckle and shot Rafe a suspicious glance.

"So what's with the white clothes?" she asked as she sat back in her seat, her tingling awareness of him making her even less tactful than usual. "A Mr. Clean complex?"

He grinned, apparently not at all offended. "I like white."

"Do you ever wear anything else?"

"Not very often," he admitted. "You might say it's been my trademark for the past four years."

"Four years?" she asked curiously. "What did you wear before that?"

"Usually black," he replied with a wry twist to his mouth. "I thought it was time for a drastic change."

A very puzzling man. She decided she needed to find out more about him. Maybe if she understood him better, she'd find him less unnerving. More ordinary.

Yeah, right.

"Have you always been in the resort business?" she asked, ignoring that mocking little voice in her head.

"No."

She waited for him to elaborate. When he didn't, she prodded impatiently, "What did you do before?"

"This and that. By the way, Tristan suggested a restaurant for us." He named it, then added, "I made reservations. Is that okay with you?"

"Yes, fine." She sighed, realizing that he had no intention of talking about his past at the moment. A good reporter knew when to back off from a line of questioning that was going nowhere.

"Tell me about your resort," she suggested over dinner at the excellent Italian restaurant Tristan had recommended. Rafe's current job seemed like a safe-enough topic of conversation. Besides, she was curious. "Tristan said you own the whole island?"

"It's a small island," Rafe confirmed with a smile. "Serendipity. Close enough to the larger islands that we can run shuttles all day for shopping and sightseeing, though many of our guests seem content to stay on Serendipity for swimming and tennis and horseback riding. At night, we run several launches to the nearby casinos, though we have our own lounge that most of our guests seem to enjoy. I've been lucky enough to book some excellent entertainers."

"Sounds like Serendipity offers a bit of everything."

"I like to think so," Rafe agreed with satisfaction. "I get very few complaints."

"It sounds heavenly. I've always wanted to visit the Caribbean."

"I think that could be arranged," Rafe murmured, watching her across the table.

She swallowed a sip of wine too quickly and just managed not to choke on it. "Maybe someday," she said vaguely, then quickly changed the subject. "How long have you been in the resort business?"

"About four years, though we've only been open for business for three. It took me over a year to get it operational."

Four years again. T.J. couldn't help wondering what other changes Rafe had made in his life four years ago. Just what *had* he done before? She made a mental note to ask Tristan if she still hadn't found out by the end of the evening. "Do you have any other plans for your resort?"

"I'd like to open another," he admitted. "I've been looking at a location in the Pacific. Eventually, I hope to have a chain of three or four resorts, though I'll probably keep my home base on Serendipity."

"Sounds very challenging," T.J. commented, though she couldn't help wondering where Rafe was getting the financing for such an ambitious plan. Setting up resorts required a large captial investment. Yet he hadn't mentioned partners and T.J. sensed that he was too much the loner, too fond of making his own decisions to rely on others. If he had partners, she suspected they were the silent kind.

"What about you?" Rafe asked, smoothly turning the conversation around. "Tristan indicated you're looking for a new job. That you haven't been happy where you are."

T.J. made a face and picked at the food on her plate. "Not lately," she concurred. "My supervisors and I don't see eye to eye on journalism ethics."

"Are you looking for a position with another newspaper?"

She shrugged discontentedly. "I don't know yet. Maybe I'll find an editorial job on a small, politically active newspaper. I wrote a political column for my college newspaper that won a few national student awards, and I wouldn't mind getting into syndication. To be honest, the whole reporting thing hasn't been what I'd hoped for when I chose my major in college."

"In what way?"

"Lots of ways. I guess I thought it was a more—oh—noble profession than it's turned out to be."

"Honest, objective journalists digging up facts that the public deserves to know? Exposing crooked politicians, keeping the clean ones on the straight and narrow?"

She gave a rather sheepish laugh at his too-close summary of her rather naive youthful fantasies. "Yeah, I guess. Turned out that even in this profession, money and power make a difference. Cover-ups, gloss-overs, lurid sensationalism—it all goes on, more than I'd expected. And there's damn little a mere reporter can do about it. After all, we have to sell those ads and subscriptions," she added bitterly.

"You remind me of some ex-cops I know," Rafe murmured. "They lost their illusions rather quickly when faced with the reality of the job. Never learned to be content with the changes they could make by working within the system or to accept that there were some things they could never change, no matter how wrong or unfair."

"Are you one of those ex-cops?" T.J. asked, trying to read his shuttered expression.

He shook his head. "Not exactly. How's your dinner?"

She swallowed a sigh at his elusiveness and looked back down at her plate. "It's very good."

"I have a chef on Serendipity who can prepare the best Italian dishes you've ever tasted. You should try his veal specialty sometime."

Again she shied away from his subtle hint that she should visit his resort, quickly changing the subject. "Have you known Tristan long?"

"Several years. How about you?"

"Three or four years, I guess. Most of the local journalists—print and broadcast—get to know each other. We met through mutual friends and then ran into each other fairly often around town, usually in the bar where he introduced us."

"You weren't at his wedding, were you? I'm sure I would have seen you."

"No. I was invited and planned to be there, but I had a last-minute assignment for the paper—back when I was covering real news," she added with a hint of bitterness. She quickly veered away from that painful topic. "So you came for the wedding?"

"I was a groomsman. It was—an interesting experience," he said with a slight smile.

She pictured Rafe in a tux and wished very much that she'd been able to attend that wedding. Would they have met then? she wondered. Would the attraction have been as immediate, as powerful, as it had been now?

She thought she'd better keep the conversation going before she embarrassed herself some way. "How did you and Tristan meet?"

"We were in South America. He was covering a military coup, I'd gotten myself in a bind. He rounded a corner just as a guerrilla terrorist put a gun to my head. A few moments later and I'd have been dead."

T.J.'s stomach clenched at Rafe's unemotional description of his close call. "What happened?" she breathed.

"Tristan shouted. The guy with the gun shot at Tristan, which gave me a chance to throw myself at him and knock him off-balance. The noise attracted attention and Tristan and I were able to get away in the ensuing confusion."

"You were both lucky to get out alive."

"Tristan took a bullet in the shoulder—the bullet that was meant for me. I'll never forget that."

T.J. suspected that Rafe would make a loyal, valuable friend—and a relentless, deadly enemy. She shivered. "What were you doing in the middle of a South American uprising?"

His smile just touched the corners of his mouth. "This and that," he murmured. "Would you like some more wine?"

T.J. frowned at him across the tiny table. "You're a very strange man, Rafe Dancer."

"Yes, I know," he replied imperturbably. "I've learned to live with it."

She couldn't help laughing. Darned if she wasn't starting to like the guy, though she was no closer to understanding him than she'd been when their eyes had met in that bar.

T.J. HAD TO STRUGGLE with the stubborn latch of her seat belt again after leaving the restaurant. Rafe's hand covered hers on the metal latch. "Let me help you with that."

T.J. froze, shaken by the feeling of having her hand trapped between his very warm skin and the cold metal buckle. "I can do it," she said in a breathless voice.

He only smiled and moved his fingers, and with a loud, metallic snap the latch locked into place. "There. That's got it."

"Um—thanks," she murmured, waiting for him to back away. His hand still covered hers and his face was only inches from her own. She couldn't help noticing what a great mouth he had—firm, nicely shaped, accented by very shallow dimples at the corners. Though that mouth had touched hers only briefly, she could remember in precise detail how it had felt. And if he didn't back away soon, she was going to attack him.

Nice going, Harris. That's really playing it cool.

She glanced up at him, to find him looking at her with a gleam of male hunger that made her tremble. Tension hummed in the air around them, building, growing, until finally T.J. could stand it no longer. She was the one who swayed forward, closing the short distance between them. Rafe didn't hesitate to take advantage of her sudden compliance. Less than a heartbeat later, he had her in his arms, his mouth moving hotly on hers.

Rafe gave her no chance to gather her defenses. He stormed her mouth, thrusting his tongue between her lips, demanding a response she was powerless to withhold from him.

She'd never thought she'd respond to the aggressive, macho approach. Yet she melted into Rafe's embrace as though she'd been waiting for him all her life. Her arms went around his neck as her mouth opened eagerly beneath his, and she found herself making a few demands of her own.

It was only a kiss, but it affected her as nothing ever had before. They were fully clothed, sitting in a public parking lot, joined by no more than their mouths and arms, and yet she felt more thoroughly claimed than when making love with those few, forgotten other men. As if something deep inside her recognized with this kiss that Tyler Jessica Harris had finally met her match.

A man who was her equal.

A man strong enough to overpower her, if she wasn't very, very careful.

That sobering thought forced its way through the haze of desire clouding her mind, and made her stiffen in Rafe's arms. She wasn't willing to risk being overpowered by any man, particularly one who was only in town for a few days!

With massive effort, she pulled away from him. "I . . . think we'd better go."

He groaned, then looked around with a frown. "You're right. This isn't the place."

Which wasn't at all what she'd meant. She took a deep, calming breath as he started the engine. She tried to ignore the demands her frustrated body still made on her. How could she say this tactfully?

Oh, the hell with tact. "I'm not going to bed with you, Rafe."

He gave her a startled look. "Is that right?"

Somehow that wasn't the response she'd expected. Watching him warily, she nodded. "I don't jump into bed with strangers. And since you're only in town for a few days . . ."

"And if I were in town for longer than a few days?" he asked casually, his attention focused on his driving.

"It wouldn't make any difference," she lied. "I'm not looking for a relationship of any sort at the moment. All my energy right now is focused on getting my career back on track. I've enjoyed the evening, but I hope you understand it ends at my door."

"Mmm."

When he didn't say anything more, she glared at him, annoyed that he was putting her in such an awkward situation. "Well?"

"Well, what?"

"Are we straight on this? You understand that I'm completely serious?"

"I heard what you said."

"Oh." She told herself she should be relieved that he wasn't making this any more difficult by trying to argue with her. He seemed to be accepting her decision easily enough. Too easily, actually. After a kiss like that, she would have expected at least a token protest! Sighing at her own inconsistency, she relaxed. "I'm glad that's settled."

He pulled the car smoothly into the parking lot of her apartment complex. "You overlooked one thing."

Her frown returned. "What thing?"

His smile was lethal, his voice pure silk. "I never asked you to go to bed with me."

She was struggling to come up with an answer when he opened his car door and stepped out, then dutifully rounded the front to open the passenger door for her. She still hadn't found anything to say when he escorted her politely to her door and left her there with nothing more than a friendly smile and a thank-you-for-the-nice-evening. No mention of calling her again.

Stunned, T.J. entered her apartment, locked the door behind her and turned on the lights. With a spurt of piqued-ego temper, she threw her purse across the room. "That arrogant, obnoxious jerk!" she snarled. "Of all the . . ."

And then she started to laugh.

Oh, yes, she was beginning to like Rafe Dancer very much, indeed. Dammit.

3

T.J. THOUGHT IT very likely that she was going to be ill. Just one more sparkling fake smile or smacking air kiss and she was going to throw up all over her too-tight, too-high shoes!

"Stop looking so disgusted, T.J.," a tall, thin man holding a camera muttered into her ear. "We're supposed to be covering this soiree, not making social or political statements about it."

"This," T.J. replied icily, glaring at the newspaper cameraman, "is the phoniest, most pretentious, most *obnoxious* group of people I have ever met in my entire life. And believe me, that's saying something!"

"I agree," Gabe whispered hastily, glancing around to make sure no one else had heard her pronouncement, "but our butts are on the line here, not to mention our jobs. So *smile*, dammit, and look like you're honored to be here."

"I'd rather—"

But the distasteful analogy would have to wait. T.J. lapsed reluctantly into discreet silence when a designer-gowned matron dripping with diamonds swooped toward her. The woman fitted right into the glittering, expensively clad crowd at this thousand-

dollar-a-ticket fund-raiser for homeless children. T.J.
wondered how any of them could swallow their own
blatant hypocrisy. And she wondered, as well, how
she'd ever force herself to write anything positive
about the phony, snobbish, painfully trendy event.

"P.J., dear, I'd like you to meet someone I know
you'll want to mention in your article," Buffy Saint
Martin trilled—a particularly annoying tone for a
woman past fifty, T.J. thought grimly. "This is Patty
Anne Delamonte from Birmingham. Her mama went
to finishing school with me. Patty Anne's here to attend my daughter's wedding this weekend—I *did*
mention that my daughter is being married in two
days, didn't I, P.J.?"

T.J. corrected her with a forced smile but knew
Buffy would never get it right, simply because she
didn't find it worth her effort to remember. "And yes,
you did mention your daughter's wedding." *Ad nau-
seum.*

During the interview T.J. had conducted with the
society leader earlier that day, Buffy had given a
complete rundown of the ostentatious wedding plans,
including the most prominent names among the six
hundred invited guests, the menu of the wedding dinner—which would most likely cost enough to feed all
the homeless children in Atlanta for at least a year—
and the couple's month-long honeymoon plans. By
the time their interview was over, T.J. had been
heartily sick of hearing about it, and sick of Buffy
Saint Martin, as well.

Sternly reminding herself that she had a job to do, T.J. dutifully took down Patty Anne's name and social standing in Birmingham, knowing Gabe would snap a picture of the two. He did, although they coyly feigned embarrassment.

"This is *such* a worthy cause," Patty Anne simpered, hoping for a quote in T.J.'s article. "Of course," she added for Buffy's benefit, "if some of those lazy homeless people would just get out and find a *job*, there really wouldn't be any problem. There's plenty of work for that sort of person—why, Jeffrey and I have been looking for a gardener for ages. And household help. Every decent maid I've hired for the past three years has been snatched by that pesky INS. And just as I was getting them to understand what I expected from them, too!"

"One just can't find decent help these days," Buffy agreed sadly, leading Patty Anne away without another glance at T.J. or Gabe. "I declare, that girl I hired last month wouldn't . . ."

Gabe hastily grabbed T.J.'s arm. "Now, T.J., calm down," he warned, looking a bit desperate as he studied her narrowed eyes and temper-warmed cheeks. "You're here to observe and take notes, remember? Not to try to educate or reform the guests!"

"I wasn't going to try to 'reform' Patty Anne," T.J. hissed, her fingers white around the pen she gripped so hard. "I was thinking about rearranging her Dior gown!"

Gabe looked after the departing duo with a raised eyebrow. "That's a Dior? I thought it looked more like an Armani."

T.J. sighed gustily. "The point is that her dress cost about five times as much as the money she donated to be seen here tonight," she snapped. "And she has the *nerve* to blame all the problems of the homeless on laziness! As though she'd pay a gardener or a maid enough to support a family or arrange for adequate child care and medical care and housing. Where does she get off?"

Gabe echoed her sigh and shook his sandy head. "Whatever was Bill thinking to assign you to the society beat?" he muttered, obviously not expecting an answer. "He's not just punishing you—he's making those of us who have to work with you suffer, too."

T.J. didn't apologize. She didn't like Gabe any more than he did her. As far as she was concerned, he was much too eager to play the games of their newpapers' new management team. If more of the staff would rebel against the tabloid-style pandering the paper was favoring lately, they might just make a difference, she thought angrily.

"I've got to get out of here," she muttered. She closed her notebook with a snap and shoved her pen into the small black purse dangling by a thin gold chain from her shoulder. "I've got enough to write an article, though God knows it's going to take a whole roll of antacids to get me through it."

"That's a good idea," Gabe agreed with visible relief. "You go on home and write up your notes. I'll just hang around here and snap a few more shots."

T.J. nodded and stalked out of the ballroom, through the lobby of the posh hotel and past a crisply uniformed doorman into the cool night air. She'd driven her own car to the affair, but had been forced to park well down the block from the entrance. She was too wrapped up in her frustration and distaste to pay much attention to her surroundings as she headed for her car.

She'd almost reached her parking place, when a rough hand grabbed the purse swinging from her shoulder, jerking her to a halt.

"Hey!" She turned furiously to find a dirty, shabbily dressed, mean-looking young tough behind her. He tugged at her purse as she instinctively pulled back at it. "Let go of that, you jerk!" she snarled, all her suppressed anger from the evening kicking her temper into high gear.

The thin chain snapped between them and the bag fell to the sidewalk at their feet. T.J. would have expected any proficient purse snatcher to grab it and run at that point.

Instead, he kept his pale blue eyes on her and moved purposefully forward. She noted that they stood only a few feet away from a deeply shadowed alleyway. And her assailant seemed to have intentions of dragging her into it, she realized when his gaze shifted rapidly around them.

Instinct, in addition to five years of self-defense training, made her lash out before he'd taken more than a step toward her. Her foot shot upward and slammed into his stomach, her high heel connecting in the vicinity of his navel. He grunted and made a grab for her, but she'd already turned into a side kick that caught him in the chin just as he bent into the pain from her first kick. His head snapped sideways. Her full skirt swirled around her legs.

Not wanting to press her advantage, she started to run back toward the safety of the hotel—only to stop in her tracks when a knife flashed in front of her.

"Okay, bitch," he spit, his free hand pressed to his bleeding chin. "Let's see you kick *this!*"

After a gruesome nightmare in her youth, T.J. had been informed by her parents that she had a scream that would rival a banshee's cry. She called on that defense now, screaming with all her might to draw attention to the battle being waged on the deserted street. At the same time, she kicked her shoes off and sent them flying toward her attacker, so that he was forced to duck or be struck in the face by a spike heel. She backed swiftly out of his range.

Spewing curses, he started toward her again, then froze when someone shouted from behind them. Another shout was followed by the sound of running feet. He didn't wait for a confrontation. He was gone before T.J. had regained her breath from the scream.

"You okay, lady?"

"Did he hurt you, ma'am?"

T.J. shook her head, startled to realize that her champions were two teenage boys, barely old enough to shave. Thank goodness the guy with the knife hadn't waited around, she thought with a surge of relief. One of these young men could have been seriously hurt trying to help her.

She thanked them gratefully, praised their courage and managed to refrain from hurting their young male egos by warning them against such reckless behavior in the future. She wasn't about to discourage a couple of genuinely concerned citizens after mingling with the money-obsessed, pleasure-seeking crowd in the hotel ballroom for the past two hours!

THE TELEPHONE was ringing when T.J. entered her apartment later that evening. She snatched it up before the answering machine could take the call, then wished she'd let it ring; it was probably one of her reporter friends who'd already heard about the attempted mugging. She'd spent the past hour filing a police report, describing her assailant to the best of her reporter's ability, and she was tired of talking about the incident.

She really should have let the machine take the call, she thought, even as she spoke into the receiver. "Hello?"

"T.J.? It's Rafe."

The image of a lean, dark man dressed all in white immediately replaced all thoughts of society parties and purse snatchers. "Um—hi," she said, remember-

ing with embarrassment his parting shot the night
before. "I never asked you to go to bed with me," he'd
said, after kissing her until her knees liquified. The
memory of that kiss had haunted her well into the
night.

"I'm not interrupting anything, I hope."

"No," she assured him, tossing her purse, with its
broken chain, onto the couch and sinking into a chair
beside the telephone table. "I just got in from an assignment for the paper."

"Working late on a Friday night?"

She saw no reason to mention the attempted mugging. Macho Rafe would probably just lecture her
about walking alone on the streets or something, and
she didn't particularly care to argue with him at the
moment. "Yeah. The usual grind."

"Actually, that's why I called—your work, I mean.
I read your article in the society pages this morning."

She prepared herself for the worst. "And . . . ?"

"It was very nicely done," he assured her, rather to
her surprise.

"Oh—um—thanks."

"Too bad about that typo, though."

T.J. frowned. "What typo? I don't remember a
typo."

"I'll read it to you . . . 'Mrs. Cantrell's hobbies include needlepoint, daily ballet exercises and squirrel
hunting.' *Squirrel hunting?*"

T.J. laughed. "It's not a typo," she said. "That's really what the lady said."

"Somehow those three activities just don't seem to go together. Do you suppose she wears her toe shoes while she stalks her prey? Goes *en pointe* when she spots one?"

T.J. suppressed a giggle. "You're being sexist, Rafe," she said mildly, and felt the tension at the back of her neck beginning to ease as she relaxed into the chair and concentrated on his deep, silky voice. "Women can dance, do artwork *and* hunt these days, you know. As well as a few other things that were once considered strictly male-only pursuits."

"Perhaps I *was* being sexist. Sorry. So what does T. J. Harris do for relaxation?"

Good question. It seemed that all T.J. had done in the past few years was work—and look where that had gotten her, she thought disgustedly, remembering the charity affair. "I have a brown belt in karate," she said, when her thoughts turned inevitably to the incident that had occurred afterward.

"I suppose that comes in handy in your line of work."

"You might be surprised," she murmured.

He paused a moment, then asked, "Any other fascinating hobbies?"

"None that I can think of at the moment. I suppose I'm a workaholic—or I used to be."

"And what about now?"

What now? Good question. "I'm still trying to decide."

"Sounds to me like you could use a vacation."

"You might be right," she admitted, trying to remember the last one. Must have been Christmas, she decided, when she'd visited her parents in Florida. Of course, she'd spent most of that week polishing a column she'd written for the paper—one that her editor had never run, dammit.

"I know a great place for a vacation—white sands, swaying palms, clear blue water, two excellent restaurants and a fairly decent lounge. You should try it."

Her mouth twitched at his obvious description of his own resort. "Maybe I will sometime."

"I'd personally take care that you had a good time," he offered nobly.

Her smile grew. She'd just bet he would! "I'll keep that in mind."

"Do that."

They chatted easily enough for another few minutes, then Rafe asked, "How would you like to attend a small dinner party with me tomorrow night at Tristan and Devon's house? It should be a pleasant evening."

She hesitated a moment.

"I'm only asking as a friend, of course," Rafe pointed out when she didn't immediately reply. "No nefarious purposes. After all, Tristan's your friend as well as mine."

"All right," she agreed rather abruptly. Rafe Dancer was just too interesting to miss another chance to get to know him better. He seemed to be content with being just another of her many male friends. And though she knew "friend" was hardly adequate to describe the awareness between them, she told herself it was safe enough. "What time?"

Rafe sounded rather smug when he answered. T.J. told herself it didn't matter. She could handle this. Hadn't she handled a society charity affair and an attempted purse snatching all in one evening? Surely she could survive an evening with Rafe Dancer without serious consequences.

"AND HE SAID he'd certainly like to talk to you about coming to work for him. He's a great guy, T.J., and a hell of a journalist. He liked what I showed him of your work and said he'd be interested in talking to you about doing a column—weekly, daily, however you want to plan it. This could even be your chance to get into syndication, kid."

"It definitely sounds interesting," T.J. told her brother, holding the telephone receiver to her ear as she glanced at her watch. Rafe was due to pick her up at any minute, but she didn't want to cut Andy short after he'd gone to the trouble of talking to an old college buddy who owned a recently started newspaper in South Carolina. T.J. didn't need her brother's help finding a job, of course—but it never hurt to have a few well placed contacts, she rationalized. "I appreciate this, Andy."

"Hey, I know how unhappy you've been with your job since the new management took over. Mike runs the sort of paper you'd be proud to work for. I mean, sure, he has to make an occasional compromise, but that's life, you know?"

"I know," T.J. said with a sigh. "Just promise me he's more interested in congressional voting records than congressional sexual habits, and I'd be delighted to talk to him."

"Trust me, T.J. You'll like him. Of course, his paper's still pretty new, and the newspaper industry's a tough one these days. No one can guarantee he'll survive the vicious competition. But I figure he's got as much of a chance as anyone."

"Yeah, well, that's something else about life. There are no guarantees."

"Right. So, you're interested?"

"I'm interested. Thanks, Andy. I appreciate this." Her doorbell rang. "My date's here. I have to go."

"Anyone I know?"

"No, just a friend." The doorbell rang again. "'Bye, Andy. Thanks again."

"Anytime, kid. Have fun on your date—but not too much fun."

She laughed and hung up, then hurried to answer the door. "Sorry, Rafe. My brother called and it took me a while to get off the phone."

"No problem," he assured her as he stepped inside. "You look very nice."

"Thank you." She returned his smile. Probably because of her rather perverse sense of humor, she'd chosen to wear black this evening—a silk camp shirt and soft, pleated slacks. Rafe, she noted, wasn't completely in white this time—his loosely pleated slacks were white, but his raw silk shirt was a pale ice blue that made him look very dark and handsome in contrast.

He politely declined her offer of a drink before they left, then asked, "Are you and your brother close?"

T.J. chuckled. "As long as we don't spend a great deal of time together. Ours is definitely an affection that grows stronger with absence. We're so much alike we can't avoid clashing at times."

"And your parents? Are you close to them?"

She nodded. "Yes, though I've only managed to see them two or three times a year since they moved to Florida after Dad retired. We talk quite frequently on the telephone."

"That's nice for you."

"What about you, Rafe? Are you close to your family?"

His expression seemed to close abruptly. "I have no family living," he replied.

"Oh. I'm sorry."

He nodded, then asked if she was ready to leave.

As she picked up her purse and headed for the door, T.J. mused that Rafe seemed like a man who was very much alone. And she wondered why she suddenly felt rather sorry for a man who seemed to be so competent and successful with everything he did.

4

THE "SMALL DINNER PARTY" turned out to be two couples—the hosts and Rafe and T.J. Aware that Rafe had intentionally misled her, T.J. gave him a reproving look when they arrived, then decided to relax and enjoy the evening. Tristan greeted her with his usual line of teasing banter; Devon welcomed her with a warm courtesy that made T.J. feel immediately at home. Devon was an attractive woman only a couple of years older than T.J., a wedding-gown designer who'd made quite a name for herself with her designs. T.J. didn't know Devon very well, but she'd liked her from the first.

"How's Her Highness this evening?" Rafe asked after the greetings had been exchanged.

"She smiled at me today," Tristan bragged. "Early for a first smile. The child is a genius."

Rafe smiled at T.J., which she returned a bit shakily—oh, what his rare, full smiles did to his usually stern face!—and then he turned back to the proud father. "Where is she? Not asleep already, I hope."

"Not yet. We kept her up so you and T.J. could see her."

"Well, then, lead the way," Rafe urged, clapping Tristan on the shoulder.

Five-week-old Courtney Elise Parrish lay in a padded infant carrier in the Parrish's elegant Queen-Anne-and-chintz living room. The plush carpet was littered with a diaper bag, several stuffed animals, two plastic rattles and three pastel baby blankets. T.J. bit her lower lip against a smile. How life had changed for the once footloose, reckless, commitment-shy Tristan! Not that Tristan seemed to mind. In fact, she'd never seen him look happier.

Tristan lifted the baby out of the carrier, smugly demonstrating his confident handling of her, while Devon stood smiling in the background. "Isn't she a love?"

"She's beautiful," T.J. answered honestly. She'd never been around babies much—and, to be quite honest, usually thought they were rather funny looking until they were old enough to at least sit up—but little Courtney *was* beautiful. Silky, honey-colored hair, smooth pink skin, a classic rosebud mouth, Devon's heart-shaped face and Tristan's blue eyes. A striking combination. "She's the prettiest baby I've ever seen."

Tristan beamed. "Want to hold her?"

"No," T.J. answered a bit too quickly. "Thanks, anyway."

Tristan laughed at her obvious panic. "C'mon, T.J., it's not that hard. It'll be good practice for you."

"I don't think I need any practice with that particular skill," T.J. retorted, hands clasped firmly behind her back. "I'll just admire her from a safe distance."

"I'd like to hold her again," Rafe said unexpectedly. "Hand her over, Tristan."

Tristan set his daughter into Rafe's strong arms without apparent concern. T.J. wasn't surprised. It seemed Rafe was competent at anything he attempted. His dark, masculine strength made a striking contrast to the infant's pastel fragility; his hands large and capable in comparison with her tiny grasping fingers. Again T.J. found complex Rafe Dancer entirely too appealing for her peace of mind.

She studied his smile as he looked down at the baby, and remembered how it had felt to have those lips pressed to her own. She glanced at the bundle cradled so carefully in his arms and remembered how he'd crushed her sensually against his chest. And then she swallowed a moan in response to a sudden wave of longing to feel those things again.

Honestly, Harris, have you lost your mind?

Rafe wasn't her type—bossy, macho men usually didn't appeal to her in the least. T.J. had enough problems in her life at the moment without becoming involved in a relationship, no matter how fleeting or casual—and something told her that, whatever she'd have with Rafe, it wouldn't be casual! And, most daunting of all, he made her feel things she didn't understand, feelings that confused her, disarmed her, even unnerved her a bit.

In her few brief relationships she'd always been firmly in control of her emotions. She didn't like it that Rafe could so easily jeopardize that control.

T.J. finally got up the nerve to stroke the baby's downy head and shook her head in wonder that any human being could be that tiny, that soft, that fragile. How could her parents not be utterly terrified at the responsibility of taking care of anything so small and helpless? She marveled at the complexities of parenthood and wondered if she herself would ever have the courage to attempt it.

At dinner, Tristan kept the conversation lively and amusing. Rafe responded with his own dry humor, T.J. with the sharp wit that usually served her well around her mostly male co-workers, Devon with a rather shy pleasure. T.J. thought the evening was moving along quite nicely, until Tristan brought up the one subject she would have preferred to avoid.

"So, T.J.," he commented, slicing into his first bite of the cheesecake Devon had prepared for dessert, "what's this about you beating up a mugger after the snooty charity thing you covered last night?"

Aware that Rafe's smile had disappeared and that his dark eyes were focused with narrowed intensity on her face, T.J. sighed and shook her head. "Nothing that dramatic. How did you hear about it, anyway?"

"Are you kidding? Everybody was talking about it today."

"Funny," Rafe murmured, his eyes still on T.J. "No one's mentioned it to *me*. What happened?"

"Some guy tried to grab my purse," T.J. replied airily, determined to downplay the incident. "I didn't particularly want to give it to him, so I kicked him in the stomach and took it back. Then a couple of teenagers ran up and the mugger wimped out and took off. No big deal."

"You forgot to mention that the guy was packing a knife. And that apparently he was prepared to use it on you," Tristan pointed out.

Devon gasped and covered her mouth with one hand. T.J. gave Tristan a look that should have singed his eyelashes. "I said it was no big deal, Parrish."

"Did he hurt you?" Rafe demanded, his voice gritty.

"No. Trust me, a confrontation with an incompetent thief was a lot more interesting than the interminable society charity affair I'd just left. Tristan, you wouldn't have believed how nauseating it was. I tried to give it a nice write-up, but I couldn't resist pointing out some of the more blatant hypocrisies. Don't know if they'll—"

"T.J.," Rafe interrupted bluntly, "hasn't anyone ever given you lessons in basic common sense?"

She turned slowly to face him, ignoring Tristan's muffled groan. "I beg your pardon?"

Rafe looked more than a little annoyed with her—which, as far as she was concerned, was totally unfair. She'd been the would-be victim last night, not the instigator!

"Never," he said crisply, "put your life at risk by resisting a mugger. You should have let the guy have the purse and gotten the hell out of there. You may have a brown belt in karate, but you still have no business taking on a man with a knife. Don't you know what could have happened?"

"What I *don't* know," she snapped, "is what makes *you* think you have the right to lecture me about what I should have done last night! I had the situation completely under control, and I came through with my purse and without injury. I think that speaks for itself."

"All it proves is that you got lucky," Rafe retorted. "This time. Next time you might just end up with your throat cut."

Devon made a sound of protest; Rafe gave her a look of contrition. "Sorry," he apologized—to Devon, T.J. noted furiously. "I'm only trying to make her understand how foolish it was to risk her life that way."

T.J. could have told him that she hadn't known the mugger was armed when she'd resisted initially, that she'd screamed bloody murder when she'd seen the knife, that she'd never been so relieved in her life as when she'd heard those teenagers running to her assistance. She could have—but she wouldn't. She was under no obligation to explain her actions to any man, Rafe Dancer included! And if he didn't like that, he could just . . .

"Perhaps we'd better talk about something else," Tristan interjected quickly, looking torn between amusement at the clash of wills and regret that he'd brought the subject up. "Has anyone read the latest

Dean Koontz thriller? I thought it was excellent—one of his best."

For Devon's sake, T.J. forced her seething gaze away from Rafe's stern face and followed Tristan's conversational lead. A moment later, Rafe, too, joined in, and the tension in the room slowly dissipated. T.J. knew, however, that the confrontation had only been postponed until she and Rafe were alone after dinner.

She had a few things to make very clear to him when that opportunity arose, she decided.

RAFE SLID behind the wheel of his car, closed the door, fastened his seat belt and started the engine. He waited only until T.J. was securely fastened in before backing out of the driveway. And then he launched directly into the confrontation T.J. had been expecting. "Why didn't you tell me about the mugger when I talked to you last night?"

"I didn't really think it was any of your business," she answered coolly, and steeled herself for his return shot.

"No," he admitted, his fingers flexing on the steering wheel, "it isn't really any of my business, I suppose. But, God, T.J., when I think what could have happened to you . . ."

Well, hell. She'd been expecting another macho lecture, and instead he sounded so genuinely concerned for her that she couldn't help softening a little in response. "Nothing did happen to me, Rafe," she pointed out, swallowing hard as she remembered a few tense moments when she'd been truly worried. "I'll admit I was a little scared, particularly when I realized he had a knife, but I'm quite capable of taking care of myself. I've been doing so for some time now."

"You made a police report?"

"Of course. I described the creep as well as I could— not that it will do any good."

"I just hope you'll be more careful in the future. Everyone has to be careful these days, especially a— uh—"

"A woman?" she supplied dryly when he stumbled.

"Well, yes," he acknowledged. "Call me old-fashioned if you want to—"

"You're old-fashioned."

"But," he went on, ignoring her prompt response, "I still think it's dangerous for a woman to be out alone on the streets of a big city. Surely you could have found someone to walk with you to your car."

T.J. couldn't help smiling as she thought of thin, nervous Gabe, who'd have been of little more value during the crisis than—well, than Buffy Saint Martin! "I know how to take care of myself, Rafe," she repeated. "But if it makes you feel any better, this incident will probably make me a bit more careful in the future."

"Good."

She wondered if he was this overprotective with all his friends—assuming, of course, he thought of her as a friend. She wasn't sure how she would have described their relationship. In some ways they were strangers, yet in other ways they were much, much more...

She wanted him, as she'd never wanted any other man. And, despite what he'd said as they'd parted after their first date, she knew full well that the desire building between them was not all one-sided. Rafe wanted her, too. She'd learned years earlier that it wasn't always wise to act on every fleeting desire, but she wasn't entirely sure she had the willpower to resist Rafe if he wanted more than a kiss tonight.

She was watching him from beneath her lashes, trying to weigh the risks of making love with him against the strength of her longing to do so, when he suddenly cursed beneath his breath and slammed on the brake. Anchored in her seat by the efficient tightening of her safety belt, T.J. could only hang on as Rafe twisted the steering wheel and floored the accelerator. Tires squealed in protest at the abrupt change of direction and velocity.

T.J. opened her mouth to ask what in the *hell* Rafe thought he was doing—but the words became a scream when a speeding car hurtled through the otherwise deserted intersection and missed Rafe's car by inches. The other vehicle never slowed, but disappeared into the nighttime streets with the roar of an angry-sounding engine.

The other driver had run a red light, T.J. realized dazedly. Had Rafe not reacted so quickly, they would have been broadsided—right in the passenger door. Squarely where she had been sitting.

There was a stunned silence in the rented car after Rafe brought it to a stop at the side of the road. T.J. looked at Rafe as he stared after the car that had come so close to hitting them, and gasped at the palpable fury in his expression. Had the other driver been within reach, T.J. suspected that Rafe would have come very close to violence at that moment.

She could see him struggle to bring his emotions back under control as he turned to her. His features relaxed slightly, his dark eyes lost some of the savage gleam that had sent a shiver coursing down her spine.

"Are you all right?" he demanded, looking closely at her.

T.J. nodded, her pulse racing, breath catching. "Yes. My God, Rafe, but that was close! If you hadn't gotten out of his way . . . how did you ever learn to drive like that?"

He ignored the question and with a glowering frown looked down the street where the other car had vanished. "Damn, I wish I'd gotten the license number. It happened so fast, I couldn't even give a reliable description."

"I never even saw him until he was right on top of us. You know, I could really do with a little less excitement in my life lately," T.J. complained, trying to ease the tension with a joke.

Rafe gave her a strange look. "You have had a lot of close calls lately, haven't you? Two near hit-and-runs, an attempted mugging . . ."

T.J. faked a shudder. "Don't remind me. A person could get tired of this many accidents all at once."

"Are you sure they *are* accidents?"

His question startled her. "What do you mean?"

"T.J., is there anything you aren't telling me? Something else you haven't mentioned because you don't consider it any of my business?"

Realizing what he was getting at, T.J. shook her head. "You can't think . . . Rafe, that's ridiculous."

He didn't return her smile. "Is it?"

"Of course it is! You're implying that these incidents haven't been coincidence—haven't been accidents."

He only looked at her.

"Rafe, that's absurd. Traffic accidents happen all the time, particularly in a city the size of Atlanta. And, I regret to say, so do muggings. The guy who tried to take my purse last night probably thought he'd hit on one of the rich society women who'd attended that shindig. He'd have been terribly disappointed if he'd seen the meager contents of my wallet."

"Have you been working on any sensitive assignments at the newspaper lately? Any potentially explosive exposés?"

"On the society beat? Hardly."

"You said you were put on that beat as punishment for being too vocal with your editorial staff. Have you made any enemies there? Anyone with reason to want you permanently out of the way?"

"No, nothing like that. Rafe—"

"Any rejected suitors? Ex-boyfriend with a grudge? Current boyfriend with a grudge?"

"No. I can't think of any reason anyone would want to harm me. Besides, wouldn't the guy who ran the red light have been hurt, too, if he'd barreled into us?"

"Not necessarily. Not if he knew what he was doing."

She didn't like the confidence in his tone—as though he would have known exactly how to cause a deadly "accident" without being harmed himself. "You want to tell me why you're suddenly sounding so much like a cop?"

His eyebrow lifted, but he didn't answer.

"*Were* you a cop, Rafe? Is that where you learned to drive that way, and to throw out questions as though you were interrogating a witness? Is that why you're so paranoid about a few coincidental incidents?"

"I don't much believe in coincidence—and no, I wasn't a cop. Not exactly."

"You said that before. What, exactly, were you?"

"I was with the DEA for a few years, before I got out and started the resort," he explained with obvious reluctance.

"DEA." Her eyes widened in response to his answer. "Oh." She shouldn't have been surprised really. She'd known from the beginning that Rafe had seen and done more than most men, had been intimately acquainted with the darker side of life.

She thought of his description of his first encounter with Tristan: *"We were in South America. He was covering a military coup—I'd gotten myself in a bind. He rounded a corner just as a guerrilla terrorist put a gun to my head. A few moments later and I'd have been dead."*

Now she knew what he'd been doing in South America. Why someone had wanted him dead. "No wonder you see would-be assassins behind every unexplained accident," she said lightly.

His hands flexed again on the steering wheel, restlessly, uncomfortably. "Let's just say I developed some fairly reliable instincts during my former career. And those instincts are telling me now that three near misses don't happen at random to the same person in such a short period of time."

"And I say you're being paranoid. There's no reason for anyone to try to harm me, Rafe. No reason at all."

He didn't look convinced, but he seemed to reach the conclusion that they'd get nowhere by arguing about it. He guided the car carefully back onto the street and completed the drive back to her apartment in taut, watchful silence.

She was almost amused by the manner in which he walked her to her door. She'd interviewed celebrities who'd been accompanied by hired bodyguards; Rafe's behavior during that short walk reminded her of those bodyguards. His shoulders squared, he kept one hand at her back, while his narrowed eyes swept the area as though looking for bogeyman hiding behind the bushes. She thought of teasing him about it. One look at the set of his firm jaw kept her quiet.

She didn't invite him in. He didn't wait for an invitation. He stepped through the door, kicked it shut behind them and took her into his arms. She thought fleetingly of reprimanding him for his high-handed manner. But then his mouth covered hers and she did exactly what she wanted to do—wrapped her arms around his neck, buried her fingers in his silky, midnight black hair and lost herself in his kiss.

THE OLD, FAMILIAR adrenaline rush triggered by the near miss in that intersection, still gripped him. Rafe had reacted by instinct when he'd caught a glimpse of the hurtling vehicle out of the corner of his eye. He'd automatically called on well honed reflexes and extensive experience to swing himself and T.J. out of danger. He was still furious that someone had come so close to hurting or maybe even killing her.

The thought of T.J. in danger threatened to release all the potential for violence he'd locked securely inside him for the past four years. He'd hoped it would never be necessary to release that side of him again. But if someone was trying to harm the woman in his arms...

He deepened the kiss, his tongue sweeping past her lips to arrogantly claim the sweetness beyond. He groaned in pleasure when she tilted her head to give him better access, welcoming him into her mouth with an eagerness that had his head spinning. She was slim and supple in his arms, her slender curves seemed to invite his touch. He slid his palms slowly down her back, feeling her warmth through the thin, black silk blouse, imagining how soft she would be beneath the fabric. That image sent a renewed rush of hunger through him that settled almost painfully in his groin. She pressed closer and a moan vibrated between them. His, he realized, unaware until then that he'd made the sound. His hands tightened on her gently rounded hips.

He wanted her as he'd never wanted anyone before her—not even the woman to whom he'd been so briefly and unsuccessfully married—and the intensity of his desire had little to do with the adrenaline still pumping through him. He'd once been all too familiar with the sexual hunger that often followed a violent encounter. There'd been times when he'd even given in to that hunger, though he'd rarely found it worth the emptiness and distaste that invariably followed.

This was different. T.J. was different. He'd wanted her from the first moment he'd seen her. And the need had grown with each moment he'd spent with her since.

He drew his mouth reluctantly from hers, then stared down at her. Her golden brown eyes were heavy lidded; her smooth, tanned peach skin flushed with passion. Her lower lip, dark and moist from his kisses, trembled when he ran his thumb slowly across it. Her short sable hair was appealingly tousled, as though she'd just risen from bed. He bit back another groan, fighting the urge to take her where they stood.

It wasn't just sex, he realized with growing dismay. It was much, much more. And having no experience with the emotions she roused in him, he backed off. He needed time to analyze these feelings, to decide what to do about them. They both needed that time. After all, they'd known each other less than a week.

He reached up to pull her arms gently from around his neck.

T.J.'s dazed expression cleared as she realized he was bringing the evening to an end. Rafe found some satisfaction in seeing the flash of disappointment in her expression before she masked it from him.

"Are you working tomorrow?" he asked, rather annoyed that his voice wasn't quite steady.

"No. I have most Sundays off."

"Have dinner with me?"

"I'm sorry, I can't. I have plans for tomorrow," she replied, pushing her hands into the pockets of her pleated black slacks, but not before Rafe saw the trembling she was trying to hide. T.J. was as shaken by the intensity of their kisses as he was—something else for him to think about when he left.

And then he frowned as he wondered if T.J.'s plans included another man. He had no right to ask, and no right to be furious with her if they did, but the thought of her with another man had his fists clenching in his pockets. "I'll call you," he said, taking a step toward the door.

"Have you decided how much longer you'll be here?" she asked, trying without a great deal of success to sound nonchalant. He attempted to read her expression, tried to determine how she would feel if he said he was leaving town immediately, but only her voice gave a clue that the question hadn't been a casual one.

"No." He didn't elaborate, didn't add that he wouldn't be leaving without seeing her again.

He put his hand on the doorknob, knowing he'd better leave before he did something really stupid. Like forbid her to see any man but him—and wouldn't *that* go over like a lead balloon? He paused just long enough to say, "Be careful, T.J. If you need me for anything—"

"I can take care of myself, Rafe," she broke in to assure him flatly. He wondered if she kept repeating that to convince him—or herself.

Knowing better than to argue with her now, he nodded curtly. "I hope so," he muttered. "Good night."

He stepped outside, closed the door behind him and walked without further hesitation to the rental car waiting in the parking lot. He slid into the driver's seat, shoved the key in the ignition, then rested both elbows on the steering wheel, his hands pressed to his eyes as he fought for control of the needs still raging through him.

And he'd thought a few days of vacation in Atlanta would be peaceful and restful! If only he'd known he'd meet a woman here who'd threaten to blow four years of hard-won control straight to hell.

5

"T.J., ARE YOU ALL RIGHT? You haven't touched your hamburger."

T.J., who had been deeply lost in thought, started at her friend's voice. "What? Oh, sorry, Gayle—I was just thinking about something."

"Something serious apparently," Gayle commented as she sat down beside T.J. at the tiny wrought-iron café table on her patio. There were other tables around them, all of them filled with laughing, chatting diners, but T.J. had deliberately chosen one slightly apart from the group. "You've been distracted ever since you got here this afternoon," Gayle accused gently.

"Have I?" T.J. made a grimace of apology. "Sorry. I didn't mean to spoil your party."

"You haven't spoiled my party in the least. I'm just worried about you. Even Nick said that something seems to be bothering you. Are you sure you're okay?"

"I'm fine—really."

"It's your job, isn't it? You're so unhappy there. Oh, T.J., as much as I'll miss you if you move away, I hope you can find something else soon. You deserve to be happy."

T.J. was touched by Gayle's genuine concern, though she regretted having given her friend cause to worry today. Gayle had been planning this first cookout of the season for weeks. Most of the guests were married couples T.J. had met before and felt quite comfortable with.

Gayle was justifiably proud of her beautiful home and her newly blooming gardens, but this informal gathering of friends was far different from the society events T.J. had so reluctantly attended recently. The clothing was casual, jewelry minimal, atmosphere relaxed and uncompetitive, laughter frequent and unforced. There were several other doctors among the Kennedys' guests, as well as a wealthy business magnate and a nationally syndicated cable-television talk-show host, but no one had bothered to arrange for media coverage. Had T.J. not been so distracted with thoughts of Rafe, she would have thoroughly enjoyed the afternoon.

"I'm fine, Gayle—really," she repeated firmly, forcing a smile. "And I'm not worried about my job—not at the moment, anyway."

Her blue eyes narrowing thoughtfully, Gayle cocked her head. "You obviously have *something* important on your mind. Would it have anything to do with that friend of Tristan's you've been out with twice this past week?" Since she and T.J. called each other often, she'd heard a bit about Rafe, though T.J. hadn't gone into much detail, telling Gayle only that Rafe

was an attractive, interesting man who was in town
for a brief visit.

Cool, unflappable, hot-tempered T. J. Harris hadn't
blushed since seventh grade, when Billy Weger had
boldly put his hand on her budding breast—just before she'd punched him right in the nose. Feeling her
cheeks flooding with unaccustomed heat now, she almost wished Rafe Dancer were close enough to punch.
This was all his fault!

Gayle studied T.J.'s rosy face with a stunned expression. "Well," she said after a moment. "Isn't this
interesting?"

T.J. groaned and covered her cheeks with her
hands. "I can't believe this," she muttered in self-
disgust. "What is that man doing to me?"

"Good question. What *is* he doing to you?" Gayle
asked with the avid curiosity of a longtime friend.

"He's making me crazy. I mean, I've only known
him a few days. And he'll be leaving soon, going back
to his tropical island. And even if he weren't, my life
is too much of a mess to even try to start a relationship with anyone now, much less someone like Rafe."

"But—"

"But," T.J. said with a sigh, "I can't stop thinking
about him."

"Why didn't you bring him with you today? I would
have loved to meet him."

"I thought about asking him," T.J. admitted. "But—
well, I decided I needed some time away from him."

Not that it had done her any good, she acknowledged ruefully. All day she'd thought about him, about the kisses they'd shared, about how bitterly disappointed she'd been when he hadn't even tried to carry those kisses further. As she'd lain awake during the night she'd told herself that she was glad nothing more had happened. She'd tried to convince herself that she would have resisted the temptation to go to bed with him. She'd tried—but she hadn't believed it for a minute.

"Gosh, T.J., I've never seen you like this over a guy before," Gayle commented artlessly. "He must be pretty special. What's he like?"

Special? Yes, Rafe was special, T.J. thought wistfully. But how was she to describe him to her friend? "He's very attractive. Tall, dark, elegant. He has a habit of wearing white, which looks very striking in contrast with his black hair and dark tan. He owns a resort in the Caribbean, and seems to be doing very well with it."

Gayle shook her head impatiently. "What's he *like?*" she persisted.

T.J. spread her hands helplessly. "Hopelessly macho. Overprotective. The strong, silent, rather intimidating type. He has a beautiful smile, but rarely uses it, and an easy charm that doesn't quite mask the darker side of him. He used to be a DEA agent, and I have a feeling that he was very, very good at his job. He's trying to forget those years now, but he's not being very successful at it. The first time I saw him, I thought that there were...well, that there were ghosts in his eyes."

Rather embarrassed at revealing so much of her own reactions to Rafe—even to Gayle, with whom she'd shared so much over the years—T.J. lapsed into self-conscious silence.

Gayle shook her strawberry-blond head in amazement. "He sounds very different from the men you usually go out with."

"He is. He's really not my type at all."

"Oh, I don't know," Gayle mused unexpectedly. "Maybe he is. None of those other guys stayed around long. Maybe this time you've finally met your match."

"Rafe and I would probably end up strangling each other," T.J. muttered.

Gayle didn't look convinced.

T.J. shook her head. "It doesn't matter, anyway. He's going back to his island and I'm looking for a new job. There's no future in the relationship."

"Probably not," Gayle agreed obligingly.

T.J. frowned. "There's not," she insisted. "I'd be a fool to start something that can't go anywhere."

"Yes. Probably."

"Gayle, you're not helping."

"What would you like me to say, T.J.?"

She sighed deeply. "Nothing. There's really nothing you can say." She picked up her hamburger, determined to put Rafe Dancer out of her mind—for the rest of the day, at least. "We're ignoring your guests,

Gayle. Go back to your hostessing duties. I'll finish my food, then start mingling."

"You're sure you're okay?"

"I'm sure. Look, Nick's trying to get your attention. You'd better find out what he wants."

Gayle left and before long someone else drifted over to talk to T.J. She made a determined effort to socialize for the remainder of the afternoon, smiling and laughing with what she considered a decent facsimile of her usual manner.

The party was just beginning to break up, when T.J. was reminded of the other problem in her life lately — her job.

"T.J., how much do you know about Ferrell Reimer's disappearance?" asked a cable talk-show host when T.J. joined an idly conversing cluster of guests at one corner of the large patio. "Any rumors going around the paper that haven't been made public yet?"

T.J. made a face. "The mysterious disappearance of an alleged crime boss is hardly a hot topic on the society beat," she muttered, making no effort to hide her frustration with her recent assignments. "No, I haven't heard any more about it than the rest of you probably have."

"It's just too bad," Gayle's husband Nick said with a disapproving shake of his sandy head. "Your paper's really gone downhill since the new management took over. It's so sanitized and cautious that it's hardly worth the effort of reading it. I get more in-depth coverage from TV news."

"That's what I've been trying to tell them," T.J. agreed. "Here we are in Atlanta—the very hub of television news coverage—and we're putting out a chatty little tabloid as competition. The other papers are leaving us in the dust, TV's creaming us—and the morons in charge just don't understand it."

"So why are you still there?" another man whom T.J. had known for several years, demanded with a genuinely puzzled expression. "How come you haven't gone over to the competition?"

"My editors have put out the word that I'm a troublemaker," T.J. explained, trying not to sound bitter. "That I'm a hothead with a temper that makes me unreliable on the job. I'm afraid that reputation is making it difficult for me to find anything else at the moment, at least locally. I have some good leads, though—some definite possibilities."

The wife of one of Nick's medical colleagues was an attorney who specialized in personal-injury cases. She cocked her head eagerly, and T.J. almost smiled at the avid look in the other woman's eyes. She knew quite a few attorneys, and they all got that very same look when they scented a possible lawsuit, T.J. thought with private amusement. She spoke before the attorney could ask the obvious question. "No, Bennie, I don't have proof that my editors are bad-mouthing me in the business. Only rumor."

"You get me a witness—maybe a signed memo— and we've got a lawsuit," Bennie insisted.

T.J. had no intention of going to court, so she thanked Bennie for her offer and deftly changed the subject. She had enough problems in her life without the aggravation of a lawsuit that could only enhance her reputation as a troublemaker!

T.J. HAD RATHER HOPED Rafe would call her Sunday evening. She left the Kennedys' house early, then went straight home and stayed close to the telephone until bedtime. It annoyed her greatly that she'd wasted an evening waiting for Rafe to call, and even more that she'd lost another night's sleep because she couldn't stop thinking about him. What was she doing, letting a man disrupt her life this way?

HER MOOD didn't improve during a truly miserable day at work on Monday. Not only was she not pursuing the real news, as she'd been trained to do, but she was crisply informed that her coverage of the Friday evening fund-raiser was unsatisfactory and that the story was being rewritten to reflect less "social bias."

"'Social bias'?" she repeated furiously. "Everything I wrote in that article—every inane quote—is entirely accurate."

"Perhaps," her editor, Dick Halzinger, replied condescendingly. "But you're well aware that your coverage was slanted. You made the guests appear shallow, insincere, hypocritical."

"All I did was report the facts," T.J. snapped. "It's up to the reader to form opinions about those facts."

"It's a society piece, not an editorial, Harris. Most of our biggest advertisers were in attendance at that event, some of the most prominent members of local society. The story's being reworked."

"Then do me a favor—make sure my name isn't on it!"

"Trust me," Halzinger replied with a smile that showed his dislike for the fiery reporter who'd been so unwillingly assigned to his section, "it won't be."

She had other assignments to work on, enough work to keep her at her desk for at least another hour. She didn't care. She had to get away. She snatched her purse out of her desk drawer and headed for the parking lot, her expression daring anyone to challenge her. No one tried.

She'd had it, she decided flatly as she stalked out of the building and into the deserted parking lot. She'd taken all she could take, given all she had to give. As soon as she got home, she was going to call her brother's friend in South Carolina and set up an interview as quickly as she could arrange it. It no longer mattered whether he was offering her a job because of her competence or because of his friendship with Andy. She had to make some changes in her life before she turned into a raving maniac!

She wasn't going to waste another evening waiting to hear from Rafe, either, she decided, turning her righteous anger to the other problem plaguing her at the moment. She'd grab a sandwich or something for dinner and then she'd head to the bar where she so often hung out with her male buddies. Mitchell and Hal and the other guys would understand her frustration with her job, encourage her to find something else, assure her she deserved better. She could always count on her pals for good-natured teasing, honest opinions and plenty of moral support. She needed all those things very badly today.

She tried to convince herself that she did *not* need sexy, infuriating Rafe Dancer.

She jabbed her key into the door lock of her car, then paused when she heard someone behind her calling her name. Reluctantly she looked over her shoulder, then sighed. Sean McLaughlin was one of her few good friends among her co-workers at the paper, one who'd loyally supported her and argued for her even at the risk of his own job security. No matter how badly she wanted to get away now, she couldn't ignore him if he wanted to talk to her.

She left the key dangling from the door lock, walked toward him and managed a weak smile when she met him some fifty feet from her car. "Hi, Sean. What do you need?"

"I thought I'd ask *you* that," he replied, searching her face with concerned green eyes. "I heard what Halzinger said to you. You okay?"

"I'm okay," she assured him, "just mad enough to hurt someone if I don't get away for a while. Preferably Halzinger."

Sean smiled. "He should consider himself lucky that you have such excellent control of your impulses."

"Right."

"I've got a job interview lined up in Chicago next week. The *Trib*. Want me to find out if they have any more openings?"

"Thanks, Sean, but I have a lead of my own to follow. I'll let you know if it works out."

"Good. Going to the bar tonight?"

"Yeah, I thought I would. You?"

"I'll be there."

She nodded and took a step toward her car. "See you later."

"Okay. You—"

A powerful concussion slammed into T.J.'s back and flung her forward even as the deafening roar of a fiery explosion reverberated in her ears. She collided forcefully with Sean, then struck something else—a car, she thought, just before her head made solid impact with something hard and unyielding.

She felt pain...and fear...and then nothing, as the world went black around her.

RAFE TOOK a sip of the coffee he'd just purchased, then grimaced expressively. "This is awful."

"I warned you, didn't I?" Tristan asked smugly, lounging in a plastic chair across the small table from Rafe. They sat in a cafeteria at the cable-news television station where Tristan worked as an anchor. He'd just given Rafe a thorough, behind-the-scenes tour of the facilities. "The problem is that you've become spoiled by your gourmet chefs at the resort. You've forgotten the times when even this slop would have tasted like the nectar of the gods."

"I haven't forgotten," Rafe answered quietly. "Though God knows I've tried."

Tristan's smile faded. "Still fighting the old battles, my friend?"

Rafe shrugged, his gaze focused on the cup between his hands. "Sometimes. Not as often as I did when I first got out, but still too often for comfort."

"It wasn't your fault, Rafe." Tristan had said the words many times before.

"I still tell myself that every day. Some days I even believe it."

"And the other days?"

Rafe only looked at him. Tristan's eyes were troubled, but he managed a smile for his friend's benefit, then steered the conversation in another direction. "Tell me what's going on between you and T.J.," he suggested. "I suppose she let you know what she thought of your 'common sense' remark after the two of you left our house Saturday evening?"

Rafe nodded. "Yeah. She did."

"T.J. isn't one to take criticism well."

"I noticed."

"She has a bit of a problem with temper."

"I noticed that, too."

"It doesn't appear to concern you overmuch."

Rafe swallowed another sip of his coffee. "It doesn't."

"You seem quite taken with her."

Rafe shot Tristan a look of warning.

Tristan cheerfully disregarded it. "She is rather fascinating," he went on. "Too hair-trigger and unpredictable for my taste, but I've always admired her spirit. And her mind. Her body's not half bad, either."

A grin tugged at the corners of Rafe's mouth. "No. Not half bad."

"I've wondered if she'd ever find a man who suited her rather forceful personality. It worried me at times —now that I've found Devon, I think everyone should have someone. I suppose I never thought of you and T.J. as a couple because you were never in the same place at the same time."

"Now wait a minute, Tristan. You sound like you're matchmaking."

"Trying my hand at it," Tristan admitted without shame. "How am I doing?"

Rafe chuckled and shook his head. "What's brought this on?"

Tristan's smile didn't fade, but his silver-blue eyes were serious. "I don't like to think of you brooding alone on that lovely island. I know what it's like to be alone, to live with old pain and regrets. To lie awake in the night, wishing you could change the past. You need someone to make you concentrate on the present and on the future. Someone to give you what I've found with Devon."

Tristan's words struck a wistful chord buried deeply within Rafe. He swallowed another sip of the terrible coffee and thought about how hard it had been not to call T.J. the day before. How badly he'd wanted just to hear her voice.

He'd spent a pleasant afternoon visiting in the home of Neal and Holly Archer, along with Tristan and his family, Neal's daughter and her husband and Neal's sister and brother-in-law, who were visiting from Birmingham, Alabama. The only single in a crowd of happily married couples, Rafe had wondered if they were really as happy and content as they'd seemed. He'd decided they were, and wondered if he'd ever find that sort of bond himself. It had certainly never existed with his former wife.

And children. Rafe had always liked children, though his ex-wife had expressed no interest in parenthood while they were together. He'd been surrounded by a new generation yesterday. Tristan's tiny daughter. Neal and Holly expecting their twins soon. Even Neal's sister, Liz Cassidy, was pregnant with her first child.

If men had the equivalent of a biological clock, Rafe could have sworn he'd heard a faint ticking somewhere inside him during the afternoon, and yet he'd found himself haunted again by the image of a dark-skinned, brown-eyed ten-year-old boy. A boy whose broad smile had turned to a grimace of shock and pain, then to the dull, empty stare of death.

The foam cup disintegrated in his clenched fist. He swore as lukewarm coffee splashed over his hand and across the table. He and Tristan both made a grab for napkins and swiped at the dark puddle before it could drip over the edge.

"You okay, Rafe?" Tristan asked, pushing the soggy pile of napkins to the center of the table.

"Yeah. Damn coffee's so bad it ate through the bottom of the cup."

Tristan obligingly smiled at Rafe's weak attempt at a joke. "Look, I'm sorry. I didn't mean to bring up a painful subject."

Rafe shook his head. "Don't worry about it. I appreciate your concern. As for your matchmaking— well, that seems rather unlikely."

"You sure about that? You and T.J. set off enough sparks to start a forest fire when you're together. Even Devon commented on it."

"There's an attraction," Rafe admitted. "Maybe more. But our paths lead in very different directions, and besides, I'm not sure she, or any woman, would be interested in getting involved with a burned-out ex-agent who's still battling some very ugly demons," he added quietly.

"Rafe—"

But whatever Tristan might have said was cut off when a tall, brunette co-worker stopped by the table with a worried expression in her large, dark eyes.

"Tristan, have you heard about T. J. Harris and Sean McLaughlin yet? It just came across the news desk. Everyone's talking about it."

Rafe froze at the grave tone of the woman's voice. He spoke before Tristan could, startling her with his urgency. "What happened?"

The woman looked uncertainly from Tristan to Rafe. "There was a bomb—"

Rafe erupted from his chair and caught the woman's forearm in a too-tight grip. "Is T.J. all right?"

"She's been taken to the hospital. Uh—Tristan?"

Tristan was also on his feet by now. He put a hand on Rafe's shoulder. "Where was she taken, Carol?" he asked, his mouth set in a grim, pale line.

She answered quickly, then added, "Both of them were alive at last report."

Rafe felt as though someone had kicked him in the stomach. He wanted to hear all the details, but more than anything he needed to see T.J. He turned to Tristan. "Will you take me to her?"

"Of course." Tristan pulled his car keys out of his pockets. "Thanks, Carol. We—"

But Rafe was already headed for the door and didn't hear the rest of what Tristan said to his co-worker. All he could think of was T.J., her brown eyes flashing with temper and defiance—and passion, and her slender, healthy body that fitted so perfectly into his arms.

He told himself that she must be all right. He couldn't allow himself to think otherwise.

T.J. WAS GROGGY, uncomfortable, jittery—and thoroughly irate. Not only had someone tried to blow her to bits, but now she was being poked, prodded, pricked and peered over by a veritable army of white-coated sadists all wearing identical annoying, condescending smiles.

"What about this, Tyler?" one of those sadists inquired brightly. "Does *this* hurt?"

T.J. flinched and swore. "Yes," she said between clenched teeth. "That hurts. Does that make you happy?"

"Now, Tyler," the fresh-faced young doctor, whose name tag identified him as Dr. Stewart, murmured with exaggerated sympathy, "you know we aren't trying to hurt you. We're trying to *help* you."

"Then stop calling me 'Tyler'!" she snapped, squirming on the paper-covered examination table in a vain attempt to get comfortable. "And stop poking at me."

Dr. Stewart frowned at her chart. "But it says here that your name is Tyler Jessica Harris. Do you prefer your middle name—Jessica? Jessie, perhaps?"

She barely suppressed a shudder. "T.J.," she muttered ungraciously. "Just call me 'T.J.'"

His expression cleared. "All right, if you prefer that. Now let me look at that knee."

She groaned loudly, expecting another less-than-gentle poke at a throbbing bruise.

"What are you doing to her?" a gravelly voice growled from the doorway. "Are you hurting her?"

Startled, T.J. turned her head, then winced at the resulting explosion of pain in her throbbing temple. She tried to lift her right hand to her head, but the IV needle strapped to her forearm stopped her abruptly. "Rafe," she murmured, trying to focus on him through the haze of shock and medication. "How—"

"Look, mister, you really must wait outside," a determined-looking nurse ordered as she tugged at Rafe's white sleeve in an attempt to keep him from entering the room. "We'll keep you informed about Ms. Harris's condition if you'll just—"

Rafe shrugged her off as though brushing aside a pesky fly. He crossed to T.J.'s side in three long, silent strides. The young doctor moved as if to interfere, but the expression of utter determination on Rafe's dark, set face stopped him.

To T.J.'s embarrassment, Rafe looked her over as thoroughly as any of the doctors had. She hardly appeared at her best. A large bandage covered most of her forehead and her short hair was matted with dried blood. Her left arm was covered in plaster from knuckles to elbow, her right arm connected by plastic tubing to the IV bottle that hung above the table. The rest of her body, which was barely covered by the short, thin cotton gown they'd wrapped her in, was liberally decorated with scrapes and bruises. "It looks worse than it is," she assured him gruffly, moved by the genuine concern in his dark, searching eyes.

He touched her cheek, and the unsteadiness in his fingers softened her even more. "Are you in pain?" he asked quietly.

"They've got me pumped full of drugs," she answered, evading the truth a bit. "It's making me groggy—I can't think clearly."

"You're all right?"

"I will be, I think." She tried to smile for him, the first smile she'd attempted in hours. And then, to her dismay, she felt her eyes fill with tears. She blinked them back angrily.

"T.J." Rafe leaned toward her.

The intimacy of the moment was broken by a gruff voice behind them. "You need some help getting him out of here?" the voice demanded.

Both T.J. and Rafe looked around to glare at the heavyset uniformed policeman who'd appeared in the doorway beside the nurse Rafe had ignored a moment earlier. "I told him to wait outside," the nurse reported crisply, "but he wouldn't listen."

"I want him to stay," T.J. said clearly, daring anyone to argue with her. She looked quickly at Stewart, probably the most easily intimidated person in the room. "I want him to stay," she repeated, holding his eyes with her narrowed ones.

He nodded hastily. "Yeah, sure, he can stay if you like, as long as he stays out of the way."

"I won't get in your way," Rafe assured him smoothly.

"Fine. Then there's no problem, is there, Officer?"

The officer frowned, but backed down. "Guess not. I've still got a lot of questions for you, Ms. Harris, as soon as the doctor here is through with you."

"She'll answer your questions as soon as she's rested a bit," Rafe replied.

The officer bristled at the autocratic tone, took one look at Rafe's expression and muttered that he'd be waiting outside when they were ready for him. And then he left, accompanied by the officious nurse.

Dr. Stewart cleared his throat rather awkwardly. "So, do the two of you spend a lot of time intimidating innocent bystanders?" he asked with a tentative smile.

T.J. and Rafe only looked at him. He cleared his throat again and turned hastily back to his work. "I'd like to look at this knee one more time," he murmured.

"Don't hurt her."

Steward nodded rapidly in response to Rafe's low order. "I'll do my best not to cause her any discomfort, sir."

T.J. smiled then, the annoying tears momentarily defeated. Her eyes met Rafe's and she saw amusement in them, as well as lingering concern for her. He covered her right hand with his own, wrapping his fingers warmly around hers. And for the first time since she'd learned that someone had tried to kill her with a car bomb, T.J. felt safe.

6

T.J. STIRRED and moaned. She tried to postpone the moment when she'd have to open her eyes and face the pain hovering at the edge of her consciousness, ready to pounce on her when she was fully awake. The medication was wearing off, she concluded as her head began to throb dully, her left arm to ache, her other scrapes and bruises to sting. Damn, but she was sore.

Without opening her eyes, she squirmed, trying to get more comfortable, then stopped when the movement only intensified the discomfort. Okay, so she'd lie very still. But she would *not* ask for more painkillers. She still felt groggy and hung over—probably about the same way she'd feel if she'd indulged in a three-day drinking marathon.

She didn't like having to work so hard to think, to remember. Disjointed images flashed through her mind. The explosion. The pain. The hospital. The doctors. The police. Rafe. Tristan. Gayle. An airplane. A helicopter...

Her eyes flew open as she suddenly remembered exactly where she was. Pressing her undamaged right hand against the bandage on her forehead, she looked around the elegantly appointed bedroom where she'd been sleeping for heaven only knew how long. There was an open window on the opposite wall, through which she could see the swaying tops of leafy palm trees and catch the scent of faintly salted air and fragrant tropical flowers.

Rafe's island. And she was staying in the spare bedroom of his private suite.

She could hardly remember how she'd ended up in this bed. She wore her favorite emerald silk nightshirt, but she didn't remember putting it on.

She tried to recall everything that had happened after she'd been treated in the emergency room. There'd been all those police questions—questions she couldn't answer because she'd had no earthly idea what reason anyone could have had for planting a bomb in her car—and then talk of protective custody. T.J. had flatly refused the suggestion of a safe house.

She almost smiled as she remembered the efficient, steamroller techniques Rafe had used to persuade the police that T.J. would be safe with him while they pursued their investigation. T.J. had made a token protest or two, but she'd been ignored almost as though she hadn't said a word. She blamed the damned drugs for her uncharacteristic acquiescence during the hours that followed.

She'd spent a night in a hospital room while Rafe had made travel arrangements. Gayle, although badly shaken by the near tragedy, had gone to T.J.'s to pack for the impromptu Caribbean "vacation." At T.J.'s request, Tristan had called her family before they heard the news through the media. He'd glossed over the incident as best he could and told them that she would be well cared for and protected for as long as necessary. The next T.J. had known, she'd been dozing in a first-class airline seat with Rafe sitting closely, protectively at her side. And, again, she'd felt safe.

Now, however, the shock and the medication had worn off, and she was feeling more herself. And she had some questions. Like why had no one waited until she was clearheaded and coherent before asking where she wanted to go? Why had Rafe suddenly taken charge as though he had some legitimate responsibility for her? And—most importantly of all— why was someone trying to kill her?

She didn't know what time it was, didn't know how long she'd been sleeping—for that matter, she didn't even know what day it was! Biting back a moan, she rolled to her right side, dragging the heavy cast on her left forearm with her, and decided now was as good a time as any to find out if she could stand.

She hadn't quite managed to sit up, when Rafe walked in. He didn't even bother to knock, she thought with a frown, settling back into the pillows. He was wearing his customary white—a blousy cotton shirt with the cuffs rolled back on his muscular arms and his usual loosely pleated slacks. And, though she noticed that he looked a bit tired, he walked with the rather arrogant confidence of a man on his own turf. A man who ruled that turf, T.J. thought, her frown deepening.

"You're awake," he said.

"How very observant of you."

His mouth twitched at her sarcasm. "Ah. Back to your usual sunny self, I see. I was beginning to worry about you. You've been so . . . cordial and agreeable."

T.J. looked grim. "You can stop worrying. I have a few questions for you, and I won't be so polite if I don't get some straight answers."

He nodded, his smile deepening. "Yes, that's my T.J." Before she could protest the hint of possession behind his words, or decide if she wanted to protest, he spoke again. "Before you start your questioning, is there anything you need? Food, water, pain medication?"

"No medication," she answered quickly. "I want to keep my head clear."

"All right. But don't hesitate to ask if you need something. There's no reason for you to suffer unnecessarily while you recuperate from your injuries."

"Just how bad *are* my injuries?" T.J. asked warily. She tried to remember what the doctors had told her, but there'd been so much going on at once, so much to try to understand.

Rafe's smile remained, but his eyes hardened. She knew his anger was aimed at whoever had done this to her, and she was glad that it wasn't directed at her. Rafe in a temper was more than a little intimidating even to T.J., whose own temper had been known to make grown men cringe. His voice, when he spoke, was gentle in contrast to the look in his eyes.

"You have a mild concussion. Your left arm is broken, just above the wrist. Other than that, assorted scrapes and bruises. You were very fortunate."

"Sean," T.J. said suddenly, remembering the rough collision with the other reporter. "How is he?"

Rafe took a seat on the edge of the bed, his thigh less than a foot away from her sheet-draped hip. "I talked to Tristan about an hour ago. He said to tell you McLaughlin is recovering, though it will be several days before he leaves the hospital. Since he took the full force of your forward momentum when you were thrown into him, his injuries were somewhat worse than your own. He's been assured that there will be no permanent damage, however.

"You were both lucky," he added rather tonelessly. "Because of the location of the bomb beneath your car, most of the glass and shrapnel were thrown away from where you and your friend were standing. Your injuries were caused primarily by the force of the explosion itself."

"Yeah," T.J. murmured, both distressed and relieved by the news about Sean. "Lucky."

"The bomb was set on a sixty-second timer that was activated when you put your key in the lock. Had your friend not called you away from the car, you'd have been behind the wheel when it went off. You wouldn't have survived."

T.J. swallowed, sobered by the realization of how very close she'd come to dying.

Rafe gave her a moment, then spoke again. "I know you've insisted repeatedly that you don't know why anyone would be trying to kill you . . ."

"I don't," she repeated yet again, looking into his dark, questioning eyes without blinking. "Rafe, I swear, I don't know why anyone would want me dead. Even after all that has happened, I still find it hard to believe someone really tried to kill me."

"Believe it." His words were grim. "Someone has a contract out on you."

"A contract," she repeated, dazed. "A professional hit?"

His upper lip curled. "Obviously not *that* professional, or you'd be dead by now. Too many screw-ups."

"Yeah, well, if it hadn't been for Sean, the last attempt would probably have succeeded."

"I know." He covered her right hand with his own. "The detectives in Atlanta are working on this, trying to find out who's behind it and why. In the meantime, you're safe here."

"Are you sure about that?" she asked in little more than a whisper, her eyes turning to the open window across from them.

He flicked an unconcerned glance in that direction, then looked back at her with a confidence she couldn't miss. "I'm sure," he said flatly. "Let's just say that security has always been a priority for me. My guests are safer here than they even imagine."

"I'm still not sure what I'm doing here," she admitted. "Everything happened so fast after the—the explosion. I can't really remember making decisions or discussing options."

Rafe cleared his throat. If she hadn't known better, she'd have sworn he looked a bit guilty. "I'm afraid we didn't give you many options. You were so opposed to a police safe house—and I didn't blame you on that point—and there didn't seem any place else to send you that you'd be safe. Your friend Gayle thought you should go to your parents' house in Florida...."

"No," T.J. said immediately. "I wouldn't have wanted them endangered if—well, if anyone followed me there."

"Exactly what I thought you'd say," Rafe assured her. "This was the logical place to bring you. It's well protected, out of the way enough that you probably wouldn't be followed . . . and besides," he added with a smile, "I'd been trying all week to figure out a way to get you here. I wanted to show you my island."

"I guess I should thank you for everything you've done for me," T.J. said, wishing for once she was a little more skilled in the social graces. "I do appreciate it, Rafe."

"You're welcome."

She thought of the expense involved in getting her to his island, and wondered if her insurance would cover it. "I'll need to arrange to have some money transferred here out of my savings. I don't know who paid for airfare and everything, but I—"

"It's been taken care of."

She shook her head against the pillows and tried to ignore the resulting throbbing at her temple. "No. I pay my own way. I'll expect you to charge me whatever your other lodgers are paying."

"None of my other lodgers are staying in my personal suite," Rafe pointed out gently. "You're my guest, T.J. Try to be gracious about it, will you?"

She glared at his slight smile, daring him to laugh at her. "What time is it, anyway?" she asked. It might be best to wait until she was a bit stronger to argue with him.

"Nine o'clock."

She frowned, glancing at the sunlight streaming through the window. "P.m.?" It had been ten o'clock Tuesday morning when they'd left Atlanta—as far as she could remember, at least.

"A.m.," he corrected. "It's Wednesday, T.J."

"Wednesday." She blinked, then scowled. "You gave me more of those painkillers, didn't you?"

"I didn't have to force you to take them. You were very cooperative yesterday."

She really was going to hit him if he laughed, she decided. Even if it *would* hurt her worse than it would him at the moment. "I was drugged to the gills, and you know it."

"Mmm." He covered his mouth with one hand to hide the grin he knew would only annoy her more. "I'm delighted to have you back to your usual self."

"I'm sure you are," she muttered sarcastically. "Don't you have something to do now that you're back in your kingdom?"

He inclined his head—regally. "Yes, quite a bit to do, actually. I thought I'd check on you first. I'm sure you must be hungry. I'll have someone bring you a breakfast tray. What would you like?"

"I don't need to be served in bed," T.J. insisted, tossing the sheet aside. And then, remembering that she was wearing only a thin nightshirt, she snatched it back. "If you'll give me some privacy, I'll get dressed now."

"It wouldn't hurt you to spend the day in bed," Rafe said. "If your safety hadn't been in question, you'd probably still be in the hospital."

"I can't get my strength back lying in bed," T.J. argued. "I have to get up, Rafe."

He nodded reluctantly. "All right. But promise me you won't overdo it. Give yourself time to recuperate."

"I won't overdo it," she promised. "I'm aware that doing so would be counterproductive."

He smiled. "I'm pleasantly surprised by your logic."

"Thank you so much," she returned dryly, then motioned toward the door with her good hand. "And now, if you'll excuse me . . . ?"

"Sure you don't need any help dressing? I'm pretty good with buttons and zippers and such."

"I'm sure you are. But I can manage, thank you."

"Then I'll be waiting in the other room for you. We'll have breakfast together. But don't try to rush. Take your time."

She sighed, though she resisted pointing out yet again that she really didn't need his instructions.

Rafe chuckled at her expression and bent over to brush a kiss against her mouth. She didn't melt into the sheets—but it had been a close call, she decided after he left and she started to breathe again.

BY THE TIME T.J. had showered in the luxurious bath connected to her bedroom and dressed in a loose-fitting, brightly striped knit romper with an elasti-cized waist, she was almost ready to go back to bed. It annoyed her how tired she was, just from getting up and getting dressed!

Someone had efficiently unpacked her bags. T.J. noted that Gayle had been very thorough in packing for her—she'd even included the file of tongue-in-cheek political columns T.J. had been writing to take her mind off her unsatisfactory work on the society beat. And Monday's newspaper, which had been left lying unread on T.J.'s kitchen table because she'd overslept. Tossing the file and the newspaper onto a small writing desk in one corner of the beautiful bed-room, T.J. smiled wryly. "Honestly, Gayle, why didn't you just throw in the kitchen sink while you were at it?" she murmured.

She slipped her feet into a pair of leather sandals and ran her fingers through her short hair, relieved that her casual style didn't require a lot of effort. She settled for a touch of plum eye shadow, a little blusher and a quick swipe of mascara, figuring that would be plenty of makeup for a resort setting. She wasn't exactly pleased with her battered-looking reflection, but she knew it could have been worse. She wasn't complaining, she decided as she supported the cast on her left forearm with the canvas sling the hospital had provided.

As he'd promised, Rafe was waiting in the next room, a spacious, glass-walled living room furnished in light, airy colors. The room curved into a bay, which held a small round table and four ornately carved chairs. Beyond that was a door that T.J. assumed led into a kitchen. She guessed that Rafe's bedroom was on the opposite side of the suite from the one in which she was staying. She wondered if she'd be seeing it before she left his island—and under what circumstances.

He'd been sitting in an armchair in the living area, sipping a cup of coffee and looking over some computer printouts, but he stood when she entered and studied her as she approached. "You look a bit pale," he observed. "You're sure you wouldn't like to rest awhile longer?"

"I'm hungry," she returned repressively. "Feed me."

He chuckled and held out his left arm. "I can't have you spreading word that I allow my guests to starve. It would do irreparable harm to my reputation as an attentive, gracious host."

Smiling at his teasing, she placed her right hand on the crook of his arm, determined to hide her lingering weakness from his too-sharp eyes. "Consider yourself on probation."

He lifted his gaze from the hand resting on his arm to her face, his smile enigmatic. "I'll keep that in mind," he murmured.

T.J. WAS BOTH charmed and impressed by Rafe's island. It was beautiful. Exactly what she'd always imagined a tropical resort should look like. A place straight out of her secret fantasies—palm trees, white sand beaches, masses of colorful flowers, and a tall, dark, handsome escort at her side.

Get a grip, Harris.

Rafe was unquestionably the ruler of this particular corner of the world. Bustling white-clad employees greeted Rafe with respect and gave T.J. friendly smiles and discreet curious looks. Rafe led her to the more casual of the island's two restaurants for breakfast, where he was welcomed with a deference bordering on veneration, in T.J.'s opinion. She wondered if he paid his staff highly to earn such loyalty, or whether they felt he'd somehow earned that respect.

"How many people work for you here, Rafe?" she asked, impressed by the servers, who unobtrusively helped as she tried to do everything with her right hand.

His answer made her blink in surprise. "Wow," she said. "Where do they all stay?"

"Most of them live here on the island," he explained. "There's a staff village on the west side. It's quite self-contained—a few shops, a small medical clinic, even a school, with classes for children from kindergarten through seventh grade. After that they must attend school on one of the larger islands. We run launches for them each day during the school year."

"I'm impressed."

"The system was set up by a former owner long before I owned the island. He built a resort here in the thirties, which was quite popular with the Hollywood crowd for a while. During the war, the place fell into poor repair. It limped along until the late fifties, when new owners turned it into a religious commune and tried to convert the locals to their rather eccentric beliefs. Most of the locals left the island and everything was allowed to run down. It sat abandoned for several years, until my father bought it as a real-estate investment in the early seventies. When he died, I inherited the island.

"Just over four years ago, I decided to try to turn it into a resort again. I pretty much leveled everything that was here and started fresh, using many of the same concepts the original owner had successfully utilized."

"It seems to be working," T.J. commented, though she couldn't help wondering again where Rafe was getting the capital for such a venture. Cottages, restaurants, tennis courts, swimming pools, docks, boats, a helicopter pad, riding trails, a stable—an entire village, for heaven's sake! Those things took money, *big* money. More than a DEA agent made in years—an honest agent, anyway.

She shook off that thought impatiently. Reporter's paranoia had a way of creeping up on her with no justification, she mused thoughtfully. She couldn't even imagine Rafe Dancer taking bribes or selling confiscated drugs or weapons or doing any of the illegal things a government man could do to make extra money. Something told her that Rafe had never been a man of divided loyalties—he'd choose a side and give that side his full commitment.

Rafe would make a loyal friend or employee, and a very dangerous enemy.

"T.J.? You're very quiet. Are you all right?"

She looked up at Rafe's question, noting the genuine concern in his eyes. Whoever he was, whatever he'd done, she had no reason to fear him, she decided. He had made her one of his friends for now, and Rafe Dancer took care of his friends. "I'm fine, Rafe. But I can't eat any more."

"Would you like to go back to your room and lie down?"

She shook her head impatiently. "I'm not an invalid. Stop treating me like one."

"Sorry. It's rather hard not to be concerned when you're sitting there looking so pale and battered."

She managed a smile. "I have to admit I'm feeling a little battered, but I need to get my strength back. I need to feel in control of my life again. Can you understand that?"

Looking at her soberly, he nodded. "Yes. I understand that. So what would you like to do this morning?"

"Look around, I suppose," she answered, relieved he wasn't going to argue, and that he seemed to really understand her aversion to feeling weak and helpless. "What will you be doing?"

"I'd like to give you a tour of the island, and then I need to spend some time in my office, catching up on the things that happened during the week I was gone."

One week, T.J. thought. She'd met Rafe only one week ago today. "I'm sorry your vacation was cut short because of me."

He shrugged. "I'd initially planned to return this week, anyway."

"I thought you said you were going to spend more time in Atlanta."

He gave her a smile. "That was after I met you."

She didn't know quite how to interpret that. She moistened her lower lip with the tip of her tongue. "There's really no need for you to give me a tour. I don't want to keep you from your work."

"Jeanette, my secretary, will know how to contact me if she needs me," Rafe replied. "I want to show you my island, T.J."

She nodded and gave him a smile that felt oddly shy. "All right, then. I'd like that."

The smile he gave her in return made her hands clench in her lap.

A dangerous man, this Rafe Dancer. And his smile was one of his more lethal weapons, she thought dazedly.

7

RAFE HAD TAKEN PRIDE in his resort from the beginning. It had given him tremendous satisfaction to create an idyllic refuge from the world's everyday problems; a place of bright sunlight and vivid colors so far different from the shadowed darkness of his former life. He particularly enjoyed showing off the resort to the occasional friend who visited—like Tristan, who'd brought Devon during their courtship. Rafe liked to think he'd played a small part in furthering that romance.

He found a special pleasure in showing Serendipity to T.J., for some reason. He drove one of the little white Jeeps he'd whimsically purchased to ferry guests around the resort, and he smiled as T.J. craned her head in an attempt to see everything at once.

"I love the swimming pools," she enthused. "It was very clever adding the waterfalls and gardens to make them look like natural island pools."

"I thought so," Rafe agreed.

"What's that?" she wanted to know a few minutes later.

"The health club—saunas, exercise room, aerobics classes. And that's the lounge over there. We have live music most nights for dancing. And I've booked some really good performers beginning this fall. Popular singers, several comedians, a ventriloquist and a magician. I'm looking forward to those shows myself."

"And what's over there?"

"The stables. And that path leads to the beach, where we have seaside bars, umbrellas and beach chairs, floats and snorkeling equipment."

"Lifeguards?"

"Of course."

"What's that?"

The tour took just over an hour. Rafe took care that she didn't miss anything. It felt right to have her beside him, he mused at one point, rather disturbed by the strength of that feeling.

Though he hadn't actually planned to stop, he found himself parking at the foot of the path that led up to his private bluff, the place he always went when the inner shadows threatened and he needed to be alone. He'd never taken any of his other guests there, but he wanted to take T.J., even though he couldn't help wondering if her memory would haunt him there after she had gone back to her own life.

"Feel up to a little walk?" he asked, trying to sound more casual than he felt.

"Sure. We've been riding all morning," T.J. pointed out. She glanced at the path clearly marked with a Do Not Enter sign. "I take it that warning doesn't include you?"

"I'm the one who posted it."

"Then I definitely want to see what's beyond," she said, climbing out of the Jeep. "I could never resist a No Trespassing sign."

"That's the reporter in you," Rafe accused mildly, and placed a hand at her waist to steady her as they started up the flower-lined path.

"Probably. What's at the top of this path, anyway?"

"You'll see. Watch that vine."

"I can walk, Rafe."

"Right. Sorry." He hid his smile at her exasperated tone. T.J. was obviously unaccustomed to being pampered. He'd bet she'd make a lousy patient when she was ill. Just as he did.

He reached out to lift a heavy sweep of fern fronds out of her way. He heard her gasp before the fronds had fallen back into place behind them.

"Oh, Rafe! This is beautiful."

He smiled. "Yes."

He watched her face as she stepped to the edge of the bluff and looked below them. From this, the highest point on the island, almost the entire resort was visible, a fantasy village in a fantasy setting. Beyond the colorful resort lay the beaches, and past that the ocean reflected the deep blue of the cloudless sky. Rafe had often thought that Gauguin would have been quite happy to sit in this spot and paint.

T.J. turned to smile at him. "No wonder you want to keep this to yourself."

A warm breeze swept past them, ruffling her bangs, bringing a glow to her cheeks. Sunlight reflected from her golden brown eyes, emphasizing their natural radiance. Her legs and arms, bared by the one-piece outfit, were smooth and lightly tanned and, despite her bandages and bruises, she looked slim and strong in this setting. Rafe wasn't talking about the view when he murmured, "Yes. I *would* like to keep this for myself."

Desire shot through him, hot, deep, immediate. He hadn't expected it and found himself struggling for the first time in years to keep his emotions masked behind his practiced, genial-host smile. He started to speak, tried to come up with something light and casual, but found it necessary to stop and clear his throat. And then couldn't think of anything to say.

He stared at her in silence for a long moment, watching as awareness slowly filled her eyes. Had there been any opposition there, any trepidation, he would have found the strength to resist his need to taste her—somehow. But her eyes held the same sensual yearning that was drawing him, and when he moved toward her, she met him halfway.

Her mouth was warm and responsive beneath his. Her lips parted, allowing him to deepen the kiss. He pulled her closer, only to stop, frustrated, when her cast came between them. She made a sound of impatience, pulled her arm out of the sling and supported the cast against his back, instead. He smiled against her lips and brought her fully against him.

It was the first time he'd allowed himself to hold her since he'd heard about the explosion. He'd known her such a short time, spent so few hours with her really, yet each time he thought of her close call, he broke into a sick, cold sweat.

He'd tried to tell himself he'd have felt the same way about any of his acquaintances, that he'd have hated for anyone to be endangered as T.J. had been. He'd tried to convince himself that his rage at her unknown assailants was a natural reaction to unjustified violence. But he'd spent the past two nights standing over her, guarding her, watching her sleep, and during those long, troubled hours he'd come to realize that what he felt was more than a friend's concern. Much more.

He didn't dare tell her about the hours that he'd watched her sleep, that he'd seen her so vulnerable and defenseless. Knowing T.J., she'd react with embarrassed displeasure and tell him exactly what she thought of his presumption with a few pithy phrases. Her defensive temper was just one of the things that made her so fascinating to him. T.J. was a woman of fire and spirit, courage and passion. And he wanted her as he'd never wanted any woman before her.

When the long, deep kiss ended he rested his cheek against the top of her head. He closed his eyes and just stood there, holding her, enjoying the feel of her in his arms, the slender length of her pressed snugly against his own taut, aroused form. Her cheek was buried in his shoulder, her arms wrapped around his waist. Her cast was digging into his back, but he didn't mind. Not as long as she was here, and she was safe, and she was holding him as tightly as he held her.

He felt her tremble and thought it was a reaction to their embrace. He wasn't feeling quite steady himself. Then her trembling intensified and he realized it was something else. He opened his eyes to look down at her, but her face was still buried in his shoulder. And she was trembling even harder. "T.J.? What's wrong?"

She made a muffled sound and shook her head against his shoulder, refusing to look at him.

He drew back a couple of inches, put a hand beneath her chin and gently turned her face up to look at him. He hadn't expected tears. Her eyes were flooded, her long lashes damp, though she was obviously fighting to keep from crying. Something twisted deep inside him. Something that felt very much like tenderness. "What is it, honey?"

"Don't call me 'honey,'" she muttered, swiping at her eyes with her right hand. "And it's nothing—it's stupid. I guess I'm just more tired than I thought."

He drew his thumb across her full, quivering lower lip. "Talk to me, T.J. Why are you crying?"

"I'm *not* crying! I just—I . . ." She stopped and looked away, her damp cheeks flushed, her eyes filling again. "Dammit."

"Are you in pain?" The thought made his stomach tighten. If she was hurting, he was going to see that she took the pain pills even if he had to force them down her throat.

"No. Not...not much, anyway," she answered, her voice ragged. "It's just . . . oh, hell, Rafe, I'm scared. And I hate it. I hate being afraid and not knowing what to do next."

He traced the path of one lone, escaped tear with the tip of his finger. "It's okay to be afraid, you know. Everyone is sometimes."

She gave him one quick, skeptical look. "Not you."

His brief laugh held little humor. "I've been afraid more times than you could ever imagine. You think I wasn't scared spitless when that guerrilla soldier had a gun to my head the day I met Tristan? I didn't want to die, T.J., but I was damned sure I was going to—and yeah, I was scared."

There'd been other times, too, when he'd been concerned for his life. But he didn't tell her that the most afraid he'd ever been in recent memory was when he'd heard that T.J. had been involved in a bombing. During that long, silent, tense ride to the hospital in Tristan's car, Rafe had been half-paralyzed at the thought that she might not be alive when they got to her. He didn't tell her, because he wasn't sure she was ready to hear it. And because he still hadn't decided exactly why or how she'd come to mean so much to him in such a short time.

Oh, yeah, he knew what it was to be scared. He was more than a little nervous right now.

"Nothing's going to happen to you, T.J.," he heard himself saying in a rough, gritty voice he hardly recognized. "No one's going to hurt you here. They'd have to get past me first."

Her eyes searched his face and she seemed to find some reassurance in what she saw there. But still she asked, "And when I leave here?"

He didn't want to think of her leaving, but he made himself answer. "By then, we'll know who's after you, and why. You have a lot of friends back in Atlanta, a lot of valuable contacts. None of them will stop working on this until you're out of danger."

She nodded, and blinked away the last of the tears, her emotions back under control. "If only I had a clue about who's behind this," she muttered, shoving her right hand through her wind-tossed hair. "If I could just think of something, *anything* that might help the investigation along. But I just don't know why anyone would want me dead. I really don't."

"Try not to worry about it for now. You concentrate on getting your strength back and let the authorities in Atlanta do their job, okay?"

"I'll try," she answered. "But it's not easy to stop thinking about it."

"No."

She gazed at the scenery below them for a long, quiet moment. And then she turned back to face him, looking up at him from beneath her lashes. It both amused and enchanted him that she seemed uncharacteristically shy when she spoke.

"Rafe? I don't usually fall apart like that."

"I know. You don't have to explain."

"I'm not trying to explain. I'm—well, I'm trying to thank you. For understanding, you know? And for caring."

Touched, he smiled and cupped her cheek in his hand. "You're welcome."

He brushed his lips across hers, but pulled back before the embrace could go any further. This really wasn't the time for anything else. At the moment, T.J. needed a friend. Rafe just hoped he could be patient until she needed—and wanted—more.

RAFE INSISTED that T.J. return to the suite to rest after their tour, while he spent a few hours working in his office. She didn't protest. As much as she hated to admit it, she needed the rest. Her head and arm ached, and she felt drained of energy. She refused the pain pills that made her so groggy, but consented to take a couple of acetaminophen tablets. Rafe stayed until she laid down, fully clothed, on her bed. She was asleep before he left the room.

She was awakened two hours later by a knock on the outer door to the suite. Blinking sleep from her eyes, she went to answer it, then paused with her hand on the doorknob. "Who is it?"

"Room service, Ms. Harris. Mr. Dancer ordered lunch for you."

Chiding herself for her paranoia, she looked through the peephole. A handsome, dark-haired young man in a crisp white jacket looked back at her. She opened the door. "Come in."

He smiled as he carefully carried in a covered tray. "My name's Joe. If you need anything while you're staying with us, you feel free to call me, okay?"

"Thank you, Joe."

He placed the tray on the small dining table set in the bay window overlooking the ocean. "Will this do?"

"Yes, that will be fine. Thank you. Um—will Rafe be joining me?"

"Mr. Dancer had a sandwich in his office. He usually does," Joe replied, whisking the cover from the tray to display a crisp salad, fish broiled in lemon butter and a bowl of fresh fruit. "If there's anything else you'd like, I'd be happy to get it for you, Ms. Harris."

"No, this looks wonderful," she assured him. "Thank you, Joe."

He left with a smile and another reminder that if she needed anything, all she had to do was pick up the phone and ask. T.J. was a little dazed at being so thoroughly indulged. A person could easily become used to such luxury, she decided, sitting down to eat. No wonder Rafe seemed so content with his island!

She ate every delicious bite of the meal. Afterward, feeling restless, she wandered around the suite. She thought longingly of the beautiful, waterfall-decorated pools and of the bathing suits Gayle had considerately packed for her. And then she looked at the cast on her left arm and scowled. Fat lot of good they'd do her.

Just to have something to do, she explored a bit more of Rafe's suite. She told herself that he wouldn't mind since he'd invited her to make herself at home. The kitchen was small, spotless and looked as though it was rarely used. Rafe probably ate all his meals in the restaurants, or had them served in his suite, she decided. The refrigerator held only a wide selection of soft drinks and fruit juices.

One wall of the living room consisted of bookshelves and cabinets. Rafe had a varied and interesting library of classics, bestsellers, adventure and horror novels. T.J. saw several titles she'd probably enjoy reading. A large cabinet in the center of the wall unit held an extensive entertainment center—television, VCR, stereo, CD player. He had quite a few videos stored behind other doors, mostly action films and black-and-white classics. A few of her own favorites were among the selections.

As for his taste in music—she flipped through tapes, CDs and albums, and groaned at what she found. John Denver, Barry Manilow, Helen Reddy, Chi-lites, Gladys Knight and the Pips, Smokey Robinson, The Captain and Tennille, The Carpenters. Every recording Liza Minnelli had ever made. No Springsteen, no Clapton, no Seger, no Mellencamp—not even a Garth Brooks or George Strait title in the bunch. "Oh, God," she muttered when she found albums by the Lettermen and Ferrante and Teicher included in Rafe's collection. "Elevator music."

Her dashing ex-agent had the musical soul of an accountant.

She wondered whimsically if there were any polyester leisure suits buried at the back of his closet. Not that she intended to find out, of course. She wasn't about to go into Rafe's bedroom without an invitation, and even if she was invited, she'd have to think about it a long time.

Diverse musical tastes notwithstanding, she wanted Rafe Dancer more than she'd ever wanted anything in her life, but the thought of doing anything about it scared her almost as much as knowing someone wanted to kill her. She knew that going to bed with Rafe would change her life—change *her*, perhaps—irrevocably. He was the one man who could make her surrender all control, the only one who'd ever threatened her emotions this way. The only man who'd ever made her think wistfully of vows and promises and long-term commitments. And if he did this to her after such a short time, after only a couple of dinners and a few mind-shattering kisses, she couldn't begin to imagine how making love with him would affect her!

She closed the doors of the cabinet, drifted to the glass wall of the living room and stared sightlessly out at the paradise beyond, her thoughts divided between her physical danger and emotional turmoil.

T.J. WASN'T the type to sit around and do nothing for very long. She read for a while, watched an old film she hadn't seen in years, then paced for half an hour trying to determine whether she felt up to a walk on the beach. Rafe appeared just as she decided to give it a try.

"I'm sorry I was gone so long," he apologized immediately. "Some paperwork piled up while I was gone, and the time got away from me while I was trying to catch up."

She shook her head, trying not to show how glad she was to see him. "I don't expect you to entertain me while I'm here, Rafe. I realize you have a lot to do."

"Some days more than others. Are you hungry? Would you like to eat out or have something brought in?"

"I'd like to get out," she answered quickly—too quickly, she decided almost as soon as the words had left her mouth. She really should start working on her manners, she thought ruefully, remembering how many times her poor mother had openly despaired of T.J. ever learning to be tactful. "It's not that I don't like your suite," she tried to explain. "I do—it's beautiful. I'm just not used to being inside all day."

"I understand," he assured her. "I get cabin fever easily myself. That was one of the many things my wife used to complain about. She liked being inside and I needed to be out in the fresh air as much as possible. She'd have hated living here."

T.J. forced herself to relax the fingers of her right hand, which had clenched into a fist when Rafe used the words "my wife." "You were married?"

Had he loved her? Had she died? Had she broken his heart? Had she been sweet and feminine and pliable—all the things T.J. was not and could never be? And why the hell did it matter so very damned much?

Rafe looked as though he hadn't meant to bring up this particular subject. He nodded shortly. "Yeah. For about an hour and a half, when I was barely into my twenties. She married someone else a few weeks after our divorce was final."

She wondered how long the marriage *had* lasted. She wondered if he regretted that it hadn't worked out. She wondered if he still loved his ex-wife. "No children?"

"No. We weren't married long enough to start thinking about the future. I think she has some kids now."

Was he sorry the children weren't his? Had he remained single since the divorce because he'd never gotten over his first love? She tried to think of something else to say.

Rafe made it unnecessary. "It was a long time ago," he said brusquely. "Nearly twenty years. To be honest, I can hardly remember what she looked like."

T.J. cocked her head and looked at him curiously. "How old are you, Rafe?" she asked, realizing she hadn't given his age any thought before now.

"I'm thirty-eight."

"You don't look it," she said candidly. Rafe had the slender, muscular build of a man nearly ten years his junior. His ebony hair was untouched by gray, his tanned face unlined except for shallow creases around his eyes and mouth.

He smiled, deepening those creases appealingly. "Thanks. I feel it sometimes. Especially when I think about how young you are. Twenty-six, right?"

"Right. How did you know?"

"Tristan told me. The night he introduced us. I asked."

"Oh. Why?"

His smile was teasing. "I wanted to know. I also asked if you were involved with anyone. I found it very interesting to hear that you'd sworn off men after breaking up with someone named Paul Davis. I was rather hoping to change your mind."

T.J.'s eyes widened and her cheeks felt warm. "Tristan told you that?"

"Well, no, I think it was Drisco who mentioned Davis."

That she could believe. Mitchell would find it very amusing to gossip about T.J.'s pathetic social life. She made a mental note to strangle him the minute she got back to Atlanta. "I would have thought you were above cheap gossip, Rafe," she said coolly.

He chuckled. "Looks like you were wrong. Just what did Paul Davis do that was so bad, anyway?"

"He tried to change me," she retorted sharply, challengingly.

"Then he was a fool," Rafe murmured. "Why would anyone want to change you?"

She lowered her head and picked at a bit of gauze sticking out from beneath the cast just covering the knuckles of her left hand. "Lots of people have tried. They say I'm too volatile, and outspoken, and impatient, and—"

"I think you're delightful," Rafe broke in, bringing her face up to his with a hand under her chin.

She usually disliked it when anyone did that to her. But Rafe's touch felt so good she couldn't find it in herself to protest even this rather high-handed treatment.

"Didn't you say something about dinner?" she asked, desperately trying to change the subject.

He laughed softly and brushed his lips over hers. "You have half an hour to change. Need any help? You know, those buttons and zippers and things?"

She made a face at him and stepped safely out of range of his disturbing touch. "I can manage."

He gave her a can't-blame-me-for-trying grin and turned toward his own room. "Just yell if you want me."

"Right," she muttered, firmly resisting an impulse to shout his name. She wanted him, all right. Badly. She just wondered if she was being a total idiot even to consider doing anything about it.

RAFE SEEMED to go out of his way to entertain T.J. over dinner in The Lagniappe, the more formal of the two restaurants on Serendipity. Again the staff welcomed them with a rather amusing overeagerness to please. They looked T.J. over with a barely veiled curiosity that made her suspect with sheepish pleasure that Rafe rarely entertained women. She was glad she'd taken time to put on some makeup and don a simple, yet flattering, sleeveless red dress. There was nothing she could do about the cast or the bruises, of course, but she'd made an effort to look the best she could under the circumstances.

T.J. couldn't resist teasing Rafe a bit about his exalted position. He shrugged and grinned wryly. "There are certain privileges to being the boss."

"You love it," she accused him.

"Most of the time," he admitted. "Wouldn't anyone?"

"Of course." She dipped a huge, tender prawn into spicy cocktail sauce. "I'd bet you come from a wealthy family."

His eyebrow lifted. "What makes you say that?"

"Several things. You said your father bought this island in the seventies, which meant he had the resources to do so. And you seem quite comfortable with the rather royal treatment you receive here—as though you grew up accustomed to servants and protocol."

He didn't look particularly pleased by her assessment. "Reporters," he muttered.

She only smiled. "Am I right?"

He lifted one shoulder beneath his white dinner jacket. "Yes. My family was quite well-off, for several generations back, actually. Oklahoma oil."

It didn't surprise her, though she couldn't help comparing his background with her own decidedly middle class upbringing. She shrugged off the momentary discomfort, telling herself she was glad she'd finally solved the mystery of how he'd financed his resort, as well as his plans for expanding his operation. "Neither of your parents is still living?"

"No."

"Do you have any brothers or sisters?"

"I have no immediate family still living," he replied. "I thought I'd mentioned that before."

"Oh, sorry. I guess you did."

"How's your arm?" he asked, obviously intent on changing the subject. "Still bothering you?"

T.J. didn't want to spoil the evening, so she went along with his change of topic. "The cast is an annoyance, but I guess I'll have to get used to it, since I'll be wearing it for several more weeks."

"Trust me, I know the feeling. I've broken half the bones in my body at one time or another. The casts are the worst part of the ordeal."

"Were you injured a lot in your job with the DEA?" she asked curiously, wondering just how dangerous his assignments had been.

"Sometimes," he answered vaguely. "Do you ride? We have some friendly, gentle mounts that you should be able to handle with one hand. You might enjoy taking a ride down the beach in a day or two."

So his former career was another taboo subject, along with his family and his ex-wife. Just what *would* Rafe consent to discuss with her? She found herself rather irritated by his secretiveness—a particularly frustrating trait for a reporter. "Yes, I've ridden. And you're right, I would enjoy a ride on the beach. Maybe I'll introduce myself to the horses tomorrow."

"I'll personally introduce you," he assured her. "How's your food?"

"Delicious."

"I've been very fortunate at finding excellent chefs," he told her, then launched into an amusing anecdote about some of the trials he'd had in interviewing talented, but decidedly eccentric chefs.

They talked easily enough during the remainder of the meal. Afterward they sat for a while in the lounge, listening to the music and watching the dancing. T.J. declined Rafe's invitation to dance, using the excuse that she was still a bit tired. She was tempted, but she *was* tired, and still quite sore—and much too confused by her reactions to Rafe to risk being in his arms tonight.

Too much had happened too quickly, she decided, settling into her pillows later after Rafe had sent her to bed with an admirably restrained kiss on the cheek and an assurance that she had only to call out if she needed him during the night. She hadn't had time to analyze her growing feelings for him. It was hard to imagine that they had much of a future together. He was quite settled on this island, and had no plans to leave other than to build and occasionally supervise similar resorts. Her work was elsewhere; there wasn't a great need for newspaper reporters on a tropical resort island.

But even if she could find something to productively occupy her time here, there were things that bothered her about Rafe. The darkness inside him and the secretiveness about him concerned her much, much more.

During the evening, he'd talked freely about his work, about his plans for this and future resorts. But questions about his past made him clam up tighter than any truth-evading politician she'd ever tried to pin down in an interview, and the reporter—not to mention the woman—in her simply couldn't be satisfied with his unnatural reticence.

SHE DIDN'T KNOW what had awakened her sometime in the middle of the night. Had it been a call of one of the island birds, coming through the screened window? One of the many aches and pains still nagging at her battered body? The subconscious awareness of being in a strange bed?

She blinked in the darkness and looked quickly around the room to make sure she was alone. She was, to her relief. She sank back into the pillows and shifted into a more comfortable position, muttering complaint about the awkwardness of her cast. She'd just closed her eyes again, when she heard the sound.

She opened them quickly, pushed herself upright and listened intently. Had it been a man's voice? Her heart picked up speed as a dozen unpleasant possibilities crossed her mind. Had they found her here— whoever it was who'd tried to kill her? Should she...?

But then the sound came again, and she recognized Rafe's voice. "No!" he said, sounding very far away, though she could tell he was somewhere in the suite. "*No!*"

She was out of the bed and across the room before he called out the second time. It never occurred to her not to go to him, that she might be putting herself into danger to do so. Rafe sounded as though he was in trouble, and T.J. was going to him. It was as simple as that.

The door to his bedroom stood open. She heard a muffled groan from inside. Taking a deep breath, she slipped into the doorway, poised to run—or to fight.

But Rafe was in bed, alone. She could see him in the moonlight coming through the open window beside the bed. He was a dark form against the white sheets, his chest bare, one arm thrown over his face. As she stood there, he groaned again, the sound so tormented it wrung her heart. "No," he muttered hoarsely. "Manuel, *run!*"

A nightmare. Only a bad dream. She thought she should go back to her own room, to spare them both the embarrassment of catching him in such an un-

guarded moment. But then he shifted restlessly in the
bed and made another muffled, haunted sound, and
she knew she couldn't leave him like this.

She stepped close to the bed and rested a gentle
hand on his sweat-sheened shoulder. "Rafe?"

8

RAFE CAME AWAKE with a gasp, his heart pounding in his chest, his skin slick with cold sweat, his mind filled with the echoes of gunshots and explosions and a boy's stunned, pain-wracked cry.

Damn, was his first thought. It had been months since the last dream. What had triggered this one?

He heard someone say his name and realized for the first time that he wasn't alone in the room. He rose on one elbow and glared at the slender, shadowy figure kneeling beside the bed. "What are you doing here?" he barked.

Her right hand had been extended toward him. At his curt tone, she dropped it to her side. "I'm sorry. I —"

He sighed and ran a hand through his tousled hair. "No. *I'm* sorry, T.J. It was just—well, you startled me."

"I understand," she assured him, sounding as though she really did. She started to rise. "If you're okay, I'll just go back—"

He caught her hand in his own, and pulled her back down. "Are *you* okay? You're not in pain or anything, are you?"

She shook her head. "I'm fine. I heard you calling out and I thought I should check on you."

"Oh." He didn't let go of her hand, though he avoided her eyes as he said, "Nightmare."

"Do you have them often?"

"Not as much as I used to." Thank God.

"Would you—um—like to talk about it?"

"No."

She looked as though she'd fully expected that answer. She nodded and, once again, moved as though to rise. "Then I'd better—"

"Don't go yet," he said, suddenly unwilling to release her hand. He told himself he was being a fool, ordered himself to let her go, but still he held on, his fingers wrapped tightly, almost desperately, around hers.

"I can't kneel like this much longer," she explained, her tone hard to read. "My legs are killing me."

"Oh. Sorry." He tugged until she was sitting on the edge of the bed, beside him. "Comfortable now?"

"Yes. What about you? Feeling better?"

"Yes." He tried to think of something else to say, something to excuse his keeping her here, something that would distract him from her nearness and the intimacy of being alone with her in his bedroom in the middle of the night. "Uh—you sure you're feeling okay? No discomfort from your injuries?"

"I wouldn't say that exactly," she answered, sounding rather amused. "I still feel like I ran smack into a brick wall, but I must be improving. Yesterday I felt as though a truck had run over me, then backed up and gotten me again."

He smiled at her imagery. "I'm not sure whether to commiserate with you or congratulate you on your improvement."

She shrugged. "It's very quiet here at night, isn't it?" she asked after a moment of silence, broken only by the steady sound of the ocean in the distance and the occasional call of a night bird.

"Yes. Our guests are usually very considerate."

She chuckled. "Your guests are all locked snugly in their own rooms and cottages," she said. "I don't think I've ever seen so many honeymooners all in one place."

"Serendipity does seem to draw honeymooners—and lovers," he agreed. "Very few children or singles."

"Must get a bit frustrating for you," she said, trying for nonchalance, though she didn't quite succeed. "All those women, already taken. Where do you find your own companionship?"

"I haven't really looked for 'companionship' very often during the past few years," Rafe replied, knowing exactly what she was asking. "I've taken the occasional business trip to the States, but on the whole I've been too busy with the resort and my other plans to spend much time—er—socializing."

He saw no need to add that no woman had more than passingly interested him during that time—until he'd seen T.J. in that Atlanta bar.

"Oh. So when you came to Atlanta, you—"

She stopped and looked away and he wondered why she'd sounded as though something had suddenly become clear to her. And then he realized what she'd meant. He frowned. "I went to Atlanta," he said very deliberately, "to visit my old friend Tristan and to see his new daughter. No other reason, no other plans. I wasn't looking for a woman, T.J. I didn't expect to meet you."

"Not *me*, of course, but—"

"No one," he cut in flatly. "I haven't been interested in one-night stands or empty affairs for a very long time. When—*if* I make love to a woman now, I want it to be more than just sex." He sat fully upright, the sheet draped over his thighs, and reached out a hand to touch her suspiciously warm cheek. Then he added quietly, "With you, it would be more."

He heard her breath catch. She shot him a startled—panicky?—look. "Rafe, I—"

He put his hand over her mouth. "I'm not expecting you to make any decisions tonight. I just thought you should know. I want you, T.J. I have from the first. But I won't rush you, won't ask for more than you're willing to give. If you only want a friend, then that's all I will be." It would drive him insane, of course, but he could control himself.

Somehow.

He hoped.

Her lips trembled against his fingers, and he snatched his hand back. He'd come too close to breaking his promise before the words had even faded away.

She moved restlessly on the bed, and for a moment he thought she was going to leave the room without another word. But then she turned fully to face him, her eyes clear through the shadows, her voice admirably steady. "I want you, too, Rafe. But," she added quickly, when he impulsively reached out to her, "I need to make something very clear before this goes any farther."

"What?" he asked, his mind still spinning at her admission.

"My life is really a mess right now. I think that's obvious enough," she added wryly, gesturing with her good hand toward the cast on her other arm. "My career is a shambles, I'm a wreck physically, I can't go home because someone wants me dead for some reason I can't begin to imagine. I can't trust my feelings right now, can't make any promises beyond the present—beyond tonight even. If you can be content with what we can have now, without expecting anything more from me, then there's nothing holding us back. If not—well, maybe we'd just better stick to being friends."

It was all he could do to keep from pulling her into his arms right then. Instead he found himself needing to ask, "Tell me one thing, T.J. Is it more than just sex for you, too?"

"Yes, Rafe," she whispered after a barely perceptible pause. "I don't know what it is exactly, but it's more than just sex."

He released a breath he hadn't known he was holding and pulled her gently toward him. "Good," he murmured, and then covered her mouth with his own.

T.J. WRAPPED her right arm around Rafe's neck and melted into the embrace. She was aware of an almost overwhelming sense of relief that the decision had finally been made. It seemed she'd wanted him forever, that she'd been destined for this man, this moment.

Rafe lay on her right side, his left arm under her as he bent over her, his mouth moving hungrily over hers. His right hand swept over her, heating her body through the clinging silk nightshirt. Her cast was a heavy inconvenience lying at her side, and she thought for a moment that it could be awkward, but then Rafe moved against her again and she stopped worrying about it. Rafe would take care of everything, she decided confidently, willingly surrendering control to a man for the first time in her adult life.

He kissed her until she was half-senseless, then dragged his mouth across her cheek and down her throat while she gasped for air. She closed her eyes, buried her right hand in his luxurious dark hair and concentrated on the feelings he evoked in her. He moved lower, slowly releasing the buttons of her nightshirt, pressing moist, openmouthed kisses on the skin revealed when the fabric parted. When the last button was undone, he slipped the loose sleeves down her arms and tossed the garment aside.

She heard his breath catch when the moonlight streaming through the open window illuminated her nude and trembling body. Her eyelids felt unnaturally heavy as she forced them open.

"T.J.," Rafe murmured, his voice thick, husky. "You're so beautiful."

She wasn't beautiful and she knew it, but she didn't want to argue with him now. She wasn't sure she could have spoken if she'd tried.

He lowered his head again, and her fingers tightened convulsively in his hair when his mouth closed over the hardened nipple of one straining, aching breast. She gasped as heat surged through her. He slipped a hand between her legs and her whole body arched and her toes dug into the sheet beneath her. Had she trusted her voice, she would have cried out his name.

She hadn't realized Rafe slept nude until he impatiently tossed aside the sheet that had gathered between them. His hair-roughened legs tangled with her smooth ones, his groin pressed into her bare hip. She felt the solid, pulsing evidence of his arousal and she swallowed a moan of need. Had she ever wanted anyone this much, ever *hurt* for anyone the way she did now?

Quivering at the sensations he roused with his hands and mouth, she suddenly realized how selfish she was being just laying there while he did all the work. She reached for him with her good hand, but he shook his head and caught her wrist, holding her arm at her side. "Next time," he murmured, his smile gleaming briefly in the shadows. "This one is for you."

She opened her mouth to say something, but then he lowered his head to press an intimate kiss into the dark curls between her thighs and the only sound that escaped her was a ragged sigh of delight.

Rafe interrupted their lovemaking only long enough to don a condom from the nightstand drawer, and by the time he surged upward and thrust deeply into her, T.J. was as incapable of rational thought as she was of speech. She wasn't worried about the future, wasn't concerned about her injuries or her career or would-be assassins. For now there was only Rafe and her and the sounds and scents of a tropical paradise. She found herself wishing the night would last forever even as the last semblance of reason left her in a shattering burst of pleasure so intense she all but lost consciousness.

IT WASN'T FOREVER, but it was a long time before T.J.'s mind finally cleared enough for coherent thought. She couldn't even guess at how much time *had* passed. She couldn't remember ever being so wrapped up in sensation and desire that she'd lost all objectivity. She'd always been so firmly in control—the detached observer, the rather cynical commentator. Even in love-making.

But this time had been different. Rafe had been in control from the beginning—the leader, the orchestrator, the one who'd thought first of responsibility and protection. T.J. wanted to believe she'd have thought of it if he'd forgotten. She wanted to believe it, but she didn't. She'd been so lost in wondrous pleasure that nothing else had even crossed her mind.

She couldn't decide exactly how she felt about that. In some ways it was nice to let someone else be the strong one for a change, have someone else making decisions and worrying about consequences. But in other ways she felt threatened by Rafe's strength and natural air of command. Not that she thought he'd ever turn that strength against her. She just couldn't help wondering if she was strong enough, confident enough to equal him.

Rafe lay heavily against her side, one arm draped protectively—possessively?—over her middle. His breathing was still rough edged, slowly returning to normal rate. She dimly remembered hearing his muffled shout of satisfaction, though she'd been so absorbed in her own climax that his had hardly registered with her. He'd been so thorough, so generous, so considerate a lover. No one had ever made her feel so special, so cherished, so utterly, deliciously desirable.

He lifted his head and gave her a smile that looked almost as dazed and disoriented as she still felt. "Hi."

She smiled in return, aware that her lips weren't quite steady. "Hi, yourself."

"You okay? I didn't hurt your arm, did I?"

"No, of course not." He'd been so careful, so intent on giving her nothing but pleasure.

A very special man, this Rafe Dancer.

A man who'd be very easy to love, if, of course, she was foolish enough to allow herself to do so.

He smoothed a damp strand of hair away from her forehead. "It's late. You should get some sleep."

"I'm really not very sleepy," she replied with total honesty. She'd rarely felt so wide-awake in her life, her body still thrumming with fading excitement, her mind racing with the possible consequences of the huge step they'd taken. "Are you?"

"No." He shifted to lie on his back at her right side and pulled her to rest against his shoulder, her plastered left arm draped carefully over his flat stomach. "Comfortable?"

"Mmm." She nestled her cheek into the hollow of his shoulder, feeling his heart beating steadily beneath her cheek. "Very."

"Good. Then you won't be in any hurry to move away, will you?"

She thought she'd be content to stay right where she was for the rest of the night—the rest of the week—the rest of her life. She cleared her throat lightly. "No. No hurry."

"Good." He stroked her hair and toyed with the short, damp ends. "Your hair is so soft and thick."

"So short?" she asked with a smile, anticipating his next comment. "Most guys like women with long, flowing hair, or at least hair that's longer than their own."

He shrugged beneath her. "I'm sure you wear it short because it's easier to care for and because you like it that way."

"Yes. I do."

"Then that's your business. Besides," he admitted with a chuckle, "I always had a thing for Liza Minnelli. Used to break out in a cold sweat every time she ran a hand through her bangs."

She thought of his music collection and smiled. "Rafe," she felt compelled to point out, "I don't look *anything* like Liza Minelli."

"No," he agreed, "but you have her haircut."

"So *that's* what you like about me."

"No," he said again, this time without any trace of teasing. "There are a lot of things I like about you, T.J., but none of them have anything to do with your resemblance to anyone else. You're unique. Special."

Realizing she was blushing at the compliment, T.J. was glad the lights were out. "Um—thanks. You're not bad yourself."

He chuckled. "Careful, T.J. Such extravagant flattery may go to my head."

"I wouldn't be here now if I didn't think you were special," she pointed out quietly.

His arm tightened around her shoulder. "That's nice to hear."

They lay in comfortable silence for a few minutes more and then T.J. said, "Actually you *do* remind me of someone . . ."

"Please don't say Ricardo Montalban," he muttered. "If you knew how many bad jokes I have to put up with about Mr. Roarke and 'Fantasy Island.'"

"Well, you do insist on wearing white," she said, laughing at his tone. "Can you blame them?"

"I *like* white. Who do I remind you of?"

"My brother Andy. You'd like him, I think."

"I'm sure I would. How do I resemble him? Physically?"

"No, not physically." She thought about it, uncertain how to put the resemblance into words. "Andy's very centered on what he wants and what he has to do to get it. He has an air of self-confidence that seems to make other people trust him and believe in his expertise, which helps a lot in his business as a financial consultant. He's a friendly, likable guy, but still a bit of a loner. Very self-contained."

"Sounds like you and your brother have quite a bit in common."

She nodded, a bit surprised by the observation. "Yes, I suppose we do in some ways. He's better at controlling his temper, though," she added ruefully. "He's always telling me that if I wouldn't fly off the handle so easily, I'd get along better with people. I'm sure he's right, but when I really get mad, I have a hard time remembering to be tactful and prudent."

Rafe laughed again, the sound a low rumble in the quiet of his bedroom. "Now why doesn't that surprise me?"

"Don't you ever lose your temper, Rafe?"

"Rarely," he admitted. "When I do, it's not pleasant. My sister Peggy used to call me The Hulk, after the comic book character who turned into an uncontrollable monster when he lost his temper. As I grew older, I learned to keep my temper under control most of the time."

"I didn't know you had a sister," T.J. said, frowning. "You never mentioned her."

There was a moment of silence, not a comfortable silence, this time, and then Rafe said almost reluctantly, "I had two sisters. Peggy and Marie. They died when I was thirteen."

T.J. lifted her head from his shoulder and looked at him in shock. "Both of them?"

"Yes. And my mother. They died in a fire at our home."

"Oh, Rafe, I'm so sorry. How awful for you."

"Yeah." He sighed, but seemed to relax beneath her a bit, as if it became somewhat easier to talk about it now that he'd started. "My father and I were away on an overnight trip with my Boy Scout troup. The fire happened during the night—something in the wiring apparently. My mother and my sisters died in their beds from smoke inhalation. They never had a chance to get out."

"You and your father must have been devastated," T.J. murmured, unable to imagine how she'd feel if most of her family had been taken in one horrible stroke.

"It was . . . rough," he said, the simple understatement making it clear how terrible it really had been for him. "My father was an alcoholic. At that time, he hadn't had a drink in years. Afterward—well—"

"He started drinking again?"

"Yeah. He crawled into a bottle and never came out. He died when I was nineteen. Financially, I was taken care of for life when my father died, but I've been pretty much on my own ever since."

T.J thought he'd probably been on his own a lot longer than that—since the fire, most likely. She tried to imagine how he would have felt, wondered whether he'd felt guilty that he and his father had been away when the fire had occurred. Knowing Rafe and his overdeveloped sense of responsibility, she bet that he had felt very guilty. Her good arm tightened around him. "I'm sorry, Rafe."

"It was a long time ago."

But it still hurt him. The grief was still there, inside him, raw and fresh, despite the passage of years. For some reason, she sensed that as clearly as if he'd told her. "How old were you when you got married?" she asked, wondering if he'd tried to create a new family then.

"Twenty-one. Just out of college."

"What was she like?" She didn't know if he'd tell her—wasn't even sure she wanted to know—but she had to ask.

"She was a nice girl. A year younger than me. Pretty, popular, good-natured."

T.J. had been right; she didn't really want to know this. But still she asked, "Did you love her?"

"I cared for her. I was very much attracted to her. I thought that was enough. I didn't realize it took a lot more to make a marriage work. We couldn't communicate. I told Tristan once that the words 'I do' were about the last ones my wife and I ever said to each other. That's an exaggeration, of course, but it pretty well sums it up. A year later, we knew it was over.

"She was very decent about it. She could have tried to take me for a chunk of money, since she knew I had plenty, but she didn't. She took a small settlement to help her get on her feet, but she refused alimony. Said she wanted to make her own way in life. She's done that quite well, I understand. Has a successful business of her own, a husband and a couple of kids. I hope she's happy—she deserves to be."

T.J. was inexplicably relieved to sense that there was no regret in Rafe's voice, no evidence that he still loved his ex-wife—if he ever had loved her. She suspected that he'd never allowed himself to become that deeply involved in the marriage, that the loss of his family had taught him to keep an emotional distance from others. She wondered if it was too late for him to change that deeply ingrained caution. "Were you working for the DEA when you were married?"

"Yeah. I went to work for them when I graduated college with a degree in criminal justice."

"Why DEA?"

He shrugged again. The movement flexed hard, taut muscles beneath her, making her briefly aware of their nudity and of how good it felt to be snugly entwined with him, talking so intimately. This emotional closeness was a new experience for her. Could be addictive, she thought warily.

She was beginning to wonder if he was going to answer her question, when he finally spoke. "Why? I don't know. They made the offer and it sounded interesting. I'd had several friends get involved with drugs, ruin their lives and careers. One friend died of an overdose three weeks before our college graduation ceremony. Because of the stocks and investments I'd inherited, I didn't need a big income from a career, but I wanted to do something worthwhile. Something challenging."

"I'm sure you found all the challenge you'd expected."

"And then some," he agreed grimly, though he didn't seem inclined to elaborate.

"How did your wife feel about your career?"

"Hated it. Aside from the danger involved, the job kept me away more than I was home. And even when I was at home, my mind was always on the job. I think she saw it as a rival, and maybe she was right."

"Did you—"

Rafe interrrupted before she could finish another question. "I could use some sleep now. How about you?"

She got the message clearly enough. There would be no more questions about his past or his former career. At least for now. Though there were many more things she'd have liked to know, more clues to understanding this complex man, she yielded to his obvious desire to change the subject. And besides, she *was* getting sleepy.

"Would you rest better if I went to my own bed?" she asked, knowing he'd probably need to work the next morning.

His arm tightened around her. "No. Stay with me."

She didn't argue, she had no desire to do so. She was exactly where she wanted to be, for now.

She closed her eyes and relaxed, her cheek cradled cozily on Rafe's shoulder, her broken arm resting comfortably at her side. She suddenly realized that the aches and pains that had nagged her since the explosion were hardly bothering her at all. She smiled as she thought of how much more effective Rafe's lovemaking had been than the painkillers the doctors had prescribed for her. She wouldn't mind a long-term prescription, she thought dreamily, her mind beginning to drift.

She fell asleep with that smile still playing on her lips, blissfully unaware that Rafe lay awake for the remainder of the night, staring into the darkness with tormented eyes, his arms locked tightly around the slender young woman in his arms.

9

RAFE WAS GONE when T.J. woke the next morning. Once again he'd arranged for breakfast to be brought to her. She'd just finished dressing in a pair of khaki shorts and a black T-shirt, when Joe arrived with the tray. T.J. thought it was very nice of Rafe to be so considerate, but as she ate alone at the little table in the bay window, she decided to tell him she'd really rather go to one of the restaurants for breakfast tomorrow. It was just a bit too lonely eating by herself in this beautiful, quiet suite.

As soon as she'd finished, she grabbed a pair of sunglasses and hurried outside. It was another gorgeous day in paradise, and she had no intention of spending it indoors. She glared down at the sling supporting her heavy cast, resenting yet again that she couldn't head straight for the pools or the beach. T.J. loved to swim and snorkel, would have been perfectly content to spend the entire day doing just that. As it was, she'd have to improvise.

She'd teased Rafe a little about being a single on a honeymooners' island. During the next two hours, she found out exactly how that felt. Everywhere she turned she saw lovers—holding hands, heads together, stealing kisses beneath bowers of fragrant blooms, slipping off to be alone in the little cottages arranged around the perimeter of the resort. She sighed rather wistfully and wondered why she, who'd never minded her own company before, was suddenly wishing for companionship. She couldn't even delude herself that it was just anyone's companionship she craved.

She wanted Rafe. And the extent of that wanting had her walking even faster, as though to escape a hazard she didn't quite understand.

After touring the entire resort, including the health club, gift shop and stables, she roamed down to the beach. Her sandals dangled from her right hand as she walked in the warm sand, her thoughts on Rafe and the night she'd spent with him, the things he'd told her about himself, the insights she'd gained from those glimpses of his past.

T.J. had never been in love, had always wondered if she was capable of the strong passions her friends seemed to feel for their lovers and spouses. She remembered watching Tristan muddle through his courtship with Devon, and she'd felt smug and superior because she'd never allowed anyone to turn her into such a vulnerable, emotional wreck. No one had ever mattered so much to her that she couldn't walk away without regrets when the relationship ended, or made her feel as though her heart would break if her feelings weren't returned.

Now she was beginning to wonder rather nervously if she was setting herself up for her first taste of heartache. Which meant, of course, that she simply couldn't allow herself to fall in love with Rafe Dancer. She'd enjoy being with him while it lasted, savor the time they spent together, but she wouldn't love him. She nodded once, decisively, satisfied with the strength of her conviction.

She looked up from her sober contemplation of the beach path to find Rafe standing some ten feet ahead of her, his gleaming hair ruffling in the breeze. His lazy smile made her bare toes curl into the sand beneath them, and she wondered if she was as firmly in control of her emotions as she'd believed herself to be. All it took was a smile from him to have her quivering like a tightly strung bow, a heartbeat away from throwing herself into his arms and flinging caution to the wind.

Rafe was looking more dangerous to her all the time.

AS THOUGH HE'D SENSED T.J.'s restlessness, Rafe went out of his way to keep her busy during the next three days. He introduced her to the operation of the resort, from personnel management to maintenance to purchasing and accounts payable. He showed her his plans and ideas for future resorts and seemed to value her opinions and suggestions. They took horseback rides on the beach, carried picnic lunches up to his private bluff overlooking the resort, danced in the lounge until late in the evening, cheerfully argued politics, religion, philosophy, arts and literature.

To the obvious fascination of his employees, Rafe was rarely away from T.J.'s side during those days, though her presence didn't appear to affect his performance of his job. To T.J.'s delight, he seemed able to concentrate totally on his responsibilities and enjoy her companionship at the same time. She didn't want to interfere with his duties, but she was very glad he seemed to enjoy being with her as much as she loved being with him.

He even put her to work after she showed him the file of satirical, politically oriented articles she'd written for her own entertainment.

He read each one thoroughly and laughed out loud several times. "T.J., these are good," he told her. "Really good. Why weren't they published?"

"Not from lack of trying on my part," she replied with a shrug, trying to hide how pleased she was with his approval. "I showed several of them to my editors, but they weren't interested. Too controversial, they said."

"That's absurd," Rafe said flatly, his brows drawn into a scowl. "This is exactly the sort of biting humor the public loves. And your political observations are astute, obviously based on extensive experience studying and covering the bureaucratic process and its participants."

She all but glowed in reaction to his flattery, though she tried to respond lightly. "My brother says my style resembles Lewis Grizzard with PMS."

Rafe chuckled. "I'd have said Erma Bombeck with an attitude."

"Garry Trudeau without his drawing pen?"

"Dave Barry with fangs," Rafe contributed gamely.

She'd run out of comparisons. She closed the file and set it aside. "I just tried to be T. J. Harris."

He touched her cheek. "You have no reason to want to be anyone else."

She moistened her lips and she had to clear her throat before she could respond. "I hope the editor in South Carolina agrees with you. Andy thinks this career change will be my chance to get into syndication—assuming, of course, I can convince someone to publish me first."

Rafe's smile faded at her mention of the job offer. She wondered if he was as reluctant for her to leave the island as she knew she would be when the time came. Thinking about leaving gave her an oddly hollow feeling, but she refused to dwell on it. She'd face that later, when the detectives in Atlanta let them know that it was safe for her to leave Serendipity.

"You know, T.J., there's something you could do for me while you're here," Rafe said suddenly with a glance at the closed file. "If you're not interested, just say so. I won't mind."

She looked at him questioningly. "What is it?"

"I need advertising copy for brochures to promote the resort," he explained. "I've had several requests from travel agents, wedding consultants and travel writers for more information than is available on the leaflets we've been sending out. I'd like to do a really sharp-looking brochure with nice photographs and clever copy that would entice the reader to spend some time here. I was planning on hiring an ad agency to take care of it, but I hesitated because I wanted to have some input into what the copy would say. Of course, it's not the sort of writing you enjoy doing, or that you're trained to do, but—"

"I've written plenty of advertising copy," she assured him, intrigued by the possibility of having a project that would occupy her time when Rafe was busy, as well as repay him in some small way for everything he'd done for her. "I'd be happy to work with you on this."

His smile returned. "Thanks. I'm sure you'll do a great job with it. I'll pay you for your time, of course."

"You will not."

"Of course I will. I would have paid an ad agency copywriter."

"Rafe." She planted her right fist on her hip and stared at him without blinking. "I'm trying to repay you for all you've done for me lately. Try to be gracious about it, will you?"

He smiled at her deliberate paraphrase of his words to her when she'd offered to pay for her room and

board at his resort. "I'd really like to find some way
to show my appreciation," he said.

She swallowed at the sudden gleam in his eyes, a
look she'd come to recognize quite well during the past
few days. And then she stepped toward him, her right
hand going out to him. "I'm sure you'll think of
something," she murmured huskily.

He caught her hand in his and pulled her into his
arms. "I'll damned sure try," he muttered, and covered her mouth with his own.

"WHY DO YOU USE your initials instead of your
names?" Rafe asked late that night as they lay in bed
after making love. "When did you start?"

Her cheek against his shoulder, she smiled. "I've
always answered to T.J. My parents had planned to
call me 'Tyler.' But when Andy, who was five and in
kindergarten when I was born, heard my names, he
refused to use either of them. He's the one who started
calling me 'T.J.' It wasn't long before everyone else did,
too."

"It suits you."

"Andy and I think so, too." She tilted her head back
to look at him. "What about your name? Is Rafe short
for anything else?"

"No. Just Rafe. I don't even have a middle name."

"Your parents just liked the name?"

"My maternal grandmother," he corrected. "She'd
always wanted to name her own son Rafe, but she had
only the one daughter, my mother. Grandmother was

half Comanche. Her father's name translated to Wolf. She'd read in a baby-name book at one time that Rafe meant something like 'house wolf'—whatever the hell that means—so she thought it a fitting tribute."

"Wolf," T.J. murmured, smiling as she thought of the sleek, silent gracefulness of his walk and the dangerous tendencies she'd sensed in him from the first. "Yes, that fits you."

She wasn't at all surprised to hear about his Native American blood. It was evident in the black hair and dark eyes, as well as the sharply carved features that were only slightly softened by European lineage.

"You think so? I assure you, I'm quite domesticated."

She made no effort to hide her skepticism. "'He's mad that trusts in the tameness of a wolf,'" she quoted.

"Shakespeare. *King Lear*. Act—three?"

She laughed and shook her head. "Beats me. I don't even know why the quote popped into my head just then. It must have been hanging around in my mind ever since lit classes in college."

"And it just happened to seem appropriate to you now?"

"Mmm. I don't think you're at all tame, Rafe."

He drew her mouth to his. "Maybe not," he murmured, his lips brushing hers as they moved. "But you're safe with me, T.J. I would never hurt you."

Maybe not deliberately, she found herself thinking as she gave herself to his kiss. She couldn't help but wonder if the hurt was already inevitable, despite Rafe's assurances to the contrary.

T.J. SAT ALONE in her room late Saturday afternoon as an easy rain fell outside, watering the lush island foliage, drumming melodiously against the windows. It was the first time it had rained since she'd been on the island, other than one brief, early-morning shower that had awoken her yesterday. She and Rafe had made love slowly, deliciously, while the sounds of the rain on the windows heightened the intimacy in his shadowy bedroom.

She thought of that interlude now, as she sat alone in the room where she'd spent so little time since she and Rafe had become lovers. She was aware of a growing sense of apprehension deep inside her, and this anxiety had nothing to do with the attacks on her that had still not been solved. Her fears had to do with Rafe, and the emotions he was making her feel for him. Like desire that only grew stronger with each night they spent in each other's arms. Like a craving for him that was beginning to feel all too much like need. Like a growing respect and affection that felt all too much like love.

She stared blindly at the notepad on the desk in front of her, unable to concentrate on advertising copy when she was so busy reminding herself of all the reasons she shouldn't fall in love with Rafe Dancer, no matter how easy it would be to do so.

Aside from the fact that their careers placed such a geographical obstacle between them, there were things about Rafe's personality that loomed just as formidably between them. His deeply ingrained take-charge attitude, for one. While T.J. believed herself strong willed enough to match him—most of the time—she knew she'd have to stay on her toes to make sure she did. She had no interest in a relationship in which she was anything less than an equal partner, nor did she think Rafe would be satisfied for long by a woman who was not as strong as he was.

And then there were those moods of his, the dark, quiet times when he seemed to be haunted by something from his past. Shadows. Ghosts. Old pain she couldn't understand.

She suspected that whatever it was had some connection to his former career, but he had utterly refused to talk about his job with the DEA. Each time she'd asked, no matter how carefully, he'd withdrawn so abruptly that she'd been hurt. Last night he'd tossed and moaned with another nightmare and called the name Manuel again. When T.J. had awakened him, he'd shied away from her concern and her questions. He'd deliberately turned his back to her for the first time in bed, leaving her to lie awake for a very long time before she'd been able to sleep again.

What kind of relationship could they have if he wasn't willing to share such an obviously important part of himself with her?

T.J. noticed that his staff respected those distant spells of his. His loyal employees seemed to watch him carefully for clues to his mood. His secretary, Jeanette, a dark-eyed, mahogany-skinned beauty whom T.J. had liked from the beginning—well, at least since she'd quickly realized that Jeanette's relationship with Rafe was strictly platonic—had hinted that T.J. should do as the rest of them did: give Rafe time and space when he fell into those moods, let him work out his problems in his own way. They rarely lasted long, Jeanette had explained. A half hour—a couple of hours at the most—and he'd be back to his usual warm, considerate, charming self.

Maybe it was her innate dislike of secrets and puzzles, but T.J. knew she'd never be able to live with those walls between her and Rafe. Because she was such an emotional person herself, it worried her a great deal that Rafe had learned to bury his feelings so effectively. He gave her passion and concern and laughter, but any deeper emotions he might have felt were kept locked away. Had been, perhaps, since he was thirteen years old.

Was Rafe even capable of loving someone fully, deeply, unreservedly? T.J. knew she would love him that way—if she allowed herself to do so, of course. And she'd never be satisfied with getting back anything less than she gave.

Trying to distract herself from that line of thinking, she pushed the blank notepad away and glanced without much interest at the week-old Atlanta newspaper still lying on one corner of the desk. There was a fuzzy photograph on the bottom of the front page, and it caught her restless attention for a moment. The man looked familiar.

Glancing at the cutline beneath the photograph, she noted the name—Ferrell Reimer. The alleged crime boss who'd disappeared around the time her own problems had begun, she realized, reaching for the newspaper. Couldn't possibly have any connection, of course, but why did he look so familiar? Maybe she should discuss this with Rafe.

The accompanying article said that Reimer had been found only hours before the newspaper had gone to press. He had been killed by a gunshot wound delivered at close range. T.J. bit her lower lip as she stared at the photo, trying to remember...

She almost jumped out of her chair when Rafe spoke from behind her. "You look lost in thought," he commented from the doorway, where he leaned comfortably against the door frame as though he'd been there watching her for some time.

She dropped the paper, promptly forgetting everything except Rafe. His hair was wet and he'd finger-combed it away from his forehead, she noticed. His white shirt and slacks were dotted with moisture and clung to the sleekly muscled frame beneath in a way that made her mouth go dry. "I thought you had some work to do," she managed to say fairly evenly.

He shrugged, his eyes locked with hers. "I did—I do. But then it started to rain, and I found myself unable to concentrate."

"Rain does that to you?"

His smile would have done a dashing pirate credit. "After yesterday morning, it does. I may never hear rain again without wanting to make love to you."

She pushed her chair back from the desk and walked over to him. "Let's hear it for monsoon season," she murmured, lifting her face to his with a smile of invitation.

He was smiling when he kissed her. "Hear, hear," he murmured, then swept her into his arms and out of the room. For just this one time, T.J. decided not to challenge his utterly macho—yet undeniably romantic—actions.

THE MARKETPLACE was crowded and noisy, a cheerful cacophony of sounds, colors, scents and enticements. Casually clad tourists from all over the world contemplated the tacky, inexpensive souvenirs as though examining rare treasures and haggled over prices in a dozen languages with exaggerated gestures. Her right hand clasped warmly in Rafe's, T.J. strolled through the pandemonium, enjoying every minute of it.

It was Sunday afternoon, and she and Rafe had come by launch from Serendipity to the nearby, larger island. Gleaming cruise ships docked in the harbor nearby discharged passengers for shopping, sight-seeing and beachcombing. The commuter planes flying constantly overhead added a few decibels to the already considerable noise level. The contrast with Serendipity's peaceful atmosphere made T.J.'s head spin.

This outing had been her idea, actually. It gave her a chance to have Rafe to herself for a few hours, away from the responsibilities of his resort. She thought it would do him good to get away from work for a few hours. His moods had grown more unpredictable each day since they'd arrived from Atlanta six days earlier, and she hoped the reason was nothing more serious than overwork.

At first Rafe hadn't been convinced that the excursion was such a good idea. He'd thought she'd be safer on Serendipity. She'd refused to listen, telling him she couldn't imagine that anyone had followed them all this way. As the days had passed, she'd begun to wonder if they'd overreacted to the threat in Atlanta. Oh, someone had definitely put a bomb beneath her car. But maybe it had been a case of mistaken identity. *Lots* of people drove beat-up blue economy cars, she reasoned. And the other incidents—the narrowly averted traffic accidents, the attempted purse snatching—well, those could be nothing more than they'd appeared.

"Right?" she'd asked Rafe, wanting very badly for him to agree with her cautiously optimistic suppositions.

Apparently he'd decided to humor her, for he'd made the arrangements for the outing. If he agreed that they might have overstated the danger she'd been in back home, he hadn't said so, to her disappointment.

"See anything you like?" Rafe asked, motioning with his free hand toward the stalls of merchandise displayed so temptingly around them. "A shell necklace? A straw bag? A throw pillow that plays 'Island Girl' when you press the center?"

She laughed and shook her head. "I just came to look this time. I'm not much of a shopper."

"What would you like to do next?"

She sighed wistfully, watching an athletic-looking young couple heading toward the beach with snorkeling gear in bags thrown over their shoulders. "I'd *like* to take a swim and do some snorkeling," she murmured enviously.

Rafe followed her glance, then looked at her broken arm. "You'll only be in that thing another five weeks," he reminded her. "Then I'll take you snorkeling. The waters around here are really beautiful. You'll love it."

And then he suddenly fell quiet, as though he'd realized that in five weeks T.J. would probably be gone. Whether her mysterious enemy had been found or not, Rafe would know that she couldn't afford to put her life on hold for much longer.

"Maybe we'll do that sometime," T.J. said lightly, though even as she spoke she wondered if they'd ever have the chance.

She couldn't imagine ever telling Rafe goodbye, but it seemed inevitable somehow. And her heart began to ache in unwilling anticipation. She sighed and looked away from him, trying to put the future out of her mind so she could enjoy the rest of the day with him.

The crowd parted suddenly and T.J. found herself staring at a shaggy-haired young man who was looking back at her with cold, angry, pale blue eyes. A faded bruise covered most of his chin, but she didn't need that to recognize him. She froze, unable for the moment to think of what to do.

"T.J.?" Rafe's curious voice broke the spell that had fallen over her as her eyes had locked with the menacing-looking young man's. "What's wrong?"

She turned to him urgently, her eyes wide and turbulent. "That guy over there—Rafe, he's the one who tried to take my purse in Atlanta!"

Rafe stiffened and his fingers tightened so suddenly around hers that she flinched. "Where?" he demanded, the word a flat, sharp snap.

She turned to point him out—then stopped.

He was gone.

"He was right there," she insisted, craning her neck to scan the crowd. Tourists and natives crowded around them in a suffocating mass, completely blocking her view. "He was standing there looking at me. I saw him."

"What does he look like?"

"Shaggy brown hair, pale blue eyes. Young. Mean."

Using the advantage of his height, Rafe spent several minutes searching the crowd for someone who matched the description. And then he looked back down at T.J. with a mixture of frustration and skepticism, which he couldn't completely hide from her. "I don't see anyone like that."

A cold chill slithered down her back. "He was there, Rafe. I know he was," she insisted, clutching his hand as though to make him believe her.

"I know you saw *someone*—"

"It was *him*. He still had the bruise on his chin where I kicked him."

Rafe muttered a curse and turned toward the harbor. "Come on."

"Where are we going?"

"Back to Serendipity."

T.J. looked over her shoulder as Rafe towed her through the bustling marketplace. "Shouldn't we tell someone? The authorities?"

Rafe didn't slow down. "Who would we tell, T.J.? And what would we tell them?"

"We—I—" She stopped, frustrated. "I don't know."

"We're going back to my island," he insisted. "I can keep you safe there."

She stopped walking, resisting his efforts to pull her along. "Rafe?"

He turned to face her, obviously impatient. "What?"

"How long am I going to be able to keep hiding there?" she whispered, searching his hard face for some clue to his thoughts. "How long can you keep watching out for me like this?"

He touched her face with fingers that were gentle in contrast with the dangerous glitter of his dark eyes. "As long as it takes to keep you safe," he said simply.

She drew a long, ragged breath and looked away from the disturbing intensity of his gaze, then allowed him to guide her to the harbor without further delay.

"IF SOMEONE HAD HER followed here, then it's someone with strings," Rafe said into the telephone receiver, the fingers of his free hand gripping a pencil.
"Serious strings. Only Tristan and the investigating
team know where she is. Keep that in mind, will you?
Yeah, I'll be waiting to hear from you."

He hung up the phone on his desk with a crash that
only partially expressed the extent of his vexation.
He'd made several calls—Tristan, the Atlanta detective leading the investigation of T.J.'s case, the government agent who owed him a big favor from the old
days—but he was growing increasingly frustrated by
the answers he was getting. Or rather, the lack of answers. The investigation was going nowhere. Someone wanted T.J. dead, but no one knew why. There
were no clues, no evidence, no known enemies.
Nothing.

Yet someone *had* tried to kill her. More than once.
And had come all too close to succeeding with the last
attempt. And now, if her imagination hadn't been
playing tricks on her in the marketplace, someone was
close to finding her again.

The pencil snapped sharply in Rafe's fist. The thought that someone meant to harm T.J. had ignited an old fury deep inside him, rekindling the violence he'd tried so hard to keep buried in the ashes of the past. Though he'd tried to hide it from her, his anger had been steadily growing during the past week. Every time he saw her fading bruises, every time she winced when her broken arm was jarred or got in her way, the need grew stronger in him to find whoever had hurt her and take his revenge.

Dimly realizing how very possessive he'd become toward her, he couldn't help thinking of how much she'd come to mean to him. He knew he frustrated her with his inability to express his emotions more fully, but he knew his feelings for her were real. Permanent. And he worried.

What did he have to offer her? An insulated life on a tropical resort, far from any city where she could pursue her career. A man with a troubled, sordid past. A man with scars so deep he doubted they'd ever heal. Who periodically went into dark moods that closed out even the people he cared most for. Who awoke in the night fighting long-dead enemies in long-departed shadows.

Just the thought of losing her, of not having her with him every day, and every night, had him breaking into a cold sweat. And paradoxically, the more he worried about losing her, the more he'd found himself drawing back from her, almost as if to prepare himself for the inevitable end.

A sound from the doorway made him look up. T.J. stood there, gazing at him soberly, no smile on her full, soft mouth, no sparkle in her striking, amber eyes. Nor did he smile in welcome. She looked serious and worried and—and vulnerable. And he knew that he'd willingly give his life to protect her if that was what it would take.

Rafe didn't take his eyes off T.J.'s troubled face as he pushed himself out of his chair. She didn't move out of the doorway as he rounded the desk and walked toward her. He reached past her and closed the door, pressing the lock as he did so. And then he placed his hands on the slender shoulders, bare except for the thin straps of her sleeveless top, and rested his forehead against hers.

"Did you find out anything?" she asked quietly, clinging to him with her one good arm.

"No."

He heard her swallow. "Oh."

"You're safe here, T.J. No one can hurt you here. Believe it, honey."

She didn't even reprimand him that time for calling her "honey." Instead, she drew a deep breath and pulled back far enough to look up at him. "Okay," she said. "What do we do next?"

God, he loved her courage. Her spirit. Her mind and body. He loved *her.* And though he wouldn't tell her, he could show her.

He lowered his mouth to hers.

T.J. seemed surprised at first, then she parted her lips and threw herself into the kiss with the eager passion he'd come to expect and to cherish. He took his time with the kiss, relishing the taste and texture of her, drawing her full lower lip between his teeth for a gentle nip and then releasing it with a soothing touch of his tongue. She trembled once, then went still in his arms, her eyes closed, her face tilted to invite more of his leisurely caresses.

He flicked the tip of his tongue into the corner of her mouth, then drew it slowly across her upper lip to the other corner, savoring the feel of her. T.J. murmured something incoherent—something that might have been his name.

He slid his hands from her shoulders down her bare forearms, loving the softness of her firm, tanned skin. His right hand encountered the heavy cast beneath her left elbow and the anger surged in him again. He forced it down, determined that this time he'd give her nothing but tenderness. It was what she needed now and what she deserved.

He abandoned her mouth for the moment and he bent his head to touch his lips to the pulse beating rapidly in her throat. Its pace increased as he lingered there, nipping, licking, tasting. His hands caressed her body, cupped her firm, rounded breasts, slid over her taut, narrow waist and slender hips to grasp the curves of her bottom and draw her against him. He made no effort to hide his arousal, but pressed her even more tightly into him so that she could feel the full, throbbing power of it. He wanted her to know what she did to him, wanted her to know how much he desired and needed her.

Her hips rotated slowly and he swallowed a groan, feeling urgency overpower the tenderness for one sharp, almost painful moment. He ruthlessly suppressed it, drawing on all the self-control he'd cultivated during his lifetime. He bent his head to taste the glistening skin of her chest, exposed by the deeply rounded neckline of her romper above the row of buttons that silently beckoned him to release them.

"Rafe." Her voice was a husky whisper. "I want you. Let's go back to your suite."

"No," he murmured, reaching for the top button, releasing it effortlessly and moving down to the next. "Here. Now."

"But what if—"

He slipped the first strap off her shoulder, then the other. "It doesn't matter."

"No—" she sighed when his mouth closed over one taut, hardened nipple "—it doesn't . . . matter . . . oh, *Rafe!*"

He bent his knees and wrapped his arms below her hips, then straightened so that her toes dangled several inches above the floor, her breasts at a level with his seeking mouth. She laughed breathlessly and caught at his shoulder with her good hand for balance. "Rafe! Put me down."

"No." He circled one pointed nipple with his tongue, then turned his attention to the other.

Her breath caught, her fingers clutched the fabric of his white shirt. Her back arched reflexively. "Rafe—"

He drew the swollen end of one breast deeply into his mouth. "Mmm?"

She moaned softly. "Don't stop."

He carried her to the deep-cushioned couch at one end of the functionally furnished office. He'd napped on that couch several times when the exhaustion of overwork had caught up with him, but he'd never shared it with anyone. Had never wanted to, until now. He laid T.J. carefully on the cushions and knelt between her raised knees.

Her long, bare legs tangled with his clothed ones. She tugged at his shirt. "I want to feel you," she said, her mouth racing across his jaw. "Take these off."

He laughed softly at the note of demand in her voice. No shy, timorous damsel, his T.J.

His shirt and slacks fell into a puddle of white on the champagne-colored carpet. Her plaid romper was a bright splash of color beside it. Both of them sighed in pleasure when bare skin finally pressed against bare skin.

He'd wanted to take his time, had intended to concentrate only on her pleasure. But desire was driving him now, the frenzy of passion overtaking him. His skin grew damp with the rigid control he exerted over himself.

T.J.'s hand swept over his body, tugging, stroking, squeezing, urging him on. Her hips moved beneath him, lifting, thrusting, taunting him with the release he craved. He slid his fingers between them and delved through the damp curls to find the swollen, wet treasure beneath. T.J. arched and gave a broken sigh of approval. His mouth raced across her face, her throat, her breasts. Then lower, to replace his hand. She gasped and went rigid, her fingers clenched in his hair.

It took every ounce of willpower he possessed to make himself wait until he felt her crest, heard her cry out her release in a thin, reedy voice. And then he surged upward, thrusting deeply into her, flinging control aside as he surrendered himself willingly to the madness.

IT WAS LONG PAST midnight that night when a muted alarm beside Rafe's bed buzzed, bringing him instantly awake. He silenced it with a touch and glanced quickly at T.J., but she still slept soundly beside him. He slid noiselessly from the bed, all the old instincts humming inside him.

Still nude, he glided into the other room and picked up the phone. He punched two digits. "What is it?" he asked a moment later.

"There's a boat approaching the south side of the island," a clipped voice answered him. "No running lights. Looks like someone's planning to come in by way of the beach."

"Let's throw a little welcoming party for them, shall we?" Rafe said smoothly, his eyes narrowing in anticipation.

The security guard chuckled. "I'll get out the party hats."

"Right. Meet you at the beach in five minutes." Rafe slid the receiver back into its cradle and slipped back into the bedroom to dress, making no sound that would rouse the woman sleeping so peacefully in his bed.

T.J. COULDN'T HAVE said what woke her. It wasn't a sound, it was more a feeling that something was wrong. She spotted movement in one corner of the bedroom and she sat upright. "What are you doing?"

Rafe stepped into the dim light coming through the window, annoyed that he'd awakened her. She was stunned to see that he was dressed all in black, and that he was sliding a deadly looking handgun into the waistband of his jeans. Her first hazy thought was that it was a good thing he usually avoided wearing dark colors; his guests would be thoroughly intimidated by their host if they saw him looking this deadly and menacing!

"What is it?" she demanded, tossing the bedcovers aside and swinging her legs over the edge of the bed. "Where are you going?"

"Only a security check," he told her, without quite meeting her eyes. "Go back to sleep, honey."

She was already stepping into the shorts Rafe had left lying on the floor beside the bed after he'd removed them from her several hours earlier. "Don't call me 'honey'—and this is no security check," she told him flatly. "Something's wrong and you're going out. I'm going with you."

"No, you're not."

She pulled a T-shirt over her head, having learned with practice to work around the cumbersome cast on her left arm. "Yes, I am," she argued, looking for her shoes. "What's happened? What are you expecting to find out there?"

"Dammit, T.J., you aren't going with me!" Rafe stepped toward her, wearing a scowl that would have dismayed anyone who didn't know him as well as T.J. did. Who didn't love him the way she did. "Someone's trying to sneak onto the island and I can only assume you're the reason. Now stay put and let me take care of this, will you?"

She'd found her shoes. Ignoring the fear that shot through her at his words, she thrust her feet into them and ran a hand through her hair. "I'm going with you, Rafe. You can't stop me."

"The hell I can't." He caught her forearm in one strong hand, his voice low and deadly. "I can lock you in this room."

Even T.J.'s nerve wavered a bit in the face of Rafe's displeasure, but that momentary lapse only made her more determined not to give in. There was no way she was going to let him put himself in danger on her behalf, not without making some effort to help him if she could. "Try it," she challenged him, drawing herself up to her full height and meeting his blazing glare without blinking.

His eyes widened for a moment as though it was the first time anyone had ever dared to defy him. And then he looked at his watch, hissed a curse between his teeth and conceded the brief clash of wills. "All right, you can come," he said reluctantly. His voice hardened. "But you will do as you're told and you will stay out of the way. Is that clear?"

"Yes," she assured him, relaxing fractionally now that he'd given in. "I won't do anything that could put us both in danger, Rafe. I promise you that."

He nodded once, curtly. "Come on, then. Stay close behind me unless I tell you otherwise."

"I will." He was already walking and she followed, her heart pounding in her throat, her bravado fading as the gravity of what they were doing sank in.

She realized, as they stepped into the fragrant darkness of the tropical night, that her fear was more for Rafe than for herself. She didn't think she'd be able to bear it if anything happened to him.

TWO ARMED security guards were waiting on the path to the south beach. Rafe gave them low-voiced instructions, which T.J. couldn't hear, then headed down the path with her close at his heels. She noted in wonder that he walked soundlessly, the animal grace she'd noticed before even more in evidence as he coolly stalked his prey.

The wolf was guarding his territory, she mused, trying to walk as quietly as he did. She'd hate to be the one who'd put that cold, deadly look in his eyes.

At the edge of the beach, Rafe stashed T.J. unceremoniously behind a tree with instructions to stay there until he told her to come out. She didn't argue, though she stood where she could see everything that was going on, fully prepared to rush in to help—broken arm and all—if Rafe appeared to be in trouble.

A few minutes later, she felt rather foolish for ever having thought that Rafe would need her assistance. Between Rafe and his guards, the two men who slipped so confidently onto the island were surrounded and disarmed almost before they realized that they'd been spotted. The capture took place so swiftly and so efficiently that Rafe's guests would never even know anything exciting had taken place within shouting distance of where they slept.

Why had she imagined that Rafe needed her here, T.J. couldn't help wondering—or that he needed her in any other way?

RAFE WAITED until the two intruders had been escorted to his offices and one of the guards dispatched to contact the police on one of the larger islands, before turning to T.J., who'd been unnaturally subdued since their clash of wills in his bedroom. "Well?" he asked her. "Either of these two look familiar?"

She nodded and glanced at the younger of the two sullen captives, who sat side by side in straight-backed chairs, their hands tied behind them, the weapons they'd carried onto the island lying on Rafe's desk only a few feet away. "That's the guy who attacked me in Atlanta. The one I saw in the marketplace."

The man she'd pointed out narrowed his pale blue eyes in menace and muttered an unflattering imprecation beneath his breath. Very calmly, very coolly, Rafe hit him. The blow caught the younger man neatly on the chin and knocked his head against the back of the chair with an audible crack. T.J. winced at the sound and stared at Rafe, wide-eyed with surprise at his actions.

He wasn't looking at her, but at the shaken, dazed man he'd just hit. "Don't call her that," Rafe advised mildly.

"Hey, wait a minute!" the angry—and obviously nervous—young man blustered. "You can't treat me like that."

"I own this island," Rafe replied with a smile that wasn't at all pleasant. "I can do anything I want."

Rafe's two muscular, white-uniformed guards glanced at each other and grinned, showing lots of teeth and implicit approval of their employer's actions. T.J. watched Rafe in amazement, finding it hard to believe how different he seemed now from the genial, mild-mannered resort host he usually appeared to be. The barely controlled wildness and the hint of savagery that she'd glimpsed in him before were very much in evidence now. And though she felt no fear of the volatile, sometimes dangerous man she'd grown to love, she could understand why others would be intimidated by him.

"Now that you understand the ground rules," Rafe said as he faced the two men with his arms crossed over the front of his black shirt, "let's have a little talk. Who sent you here? Who have you been working for?"

Neither of them answered. Instead they exchanged wary glances, the younger man looking to the older, tougher looking one for guidance. The older man shook his balding head.

Rafe cleared his throat, his eyes still focused unblinkingly on the younger of the two. "Maybe you didn't hear me," he suggested almost congenially. "I want to know who hired you to hurt my friend."

"Look," the younger man said, breaking into a sweat. "If we tell you that, we'll be dead as soon as we get back to Atlanta."

"Oh, I wouldn't worry about that if I were you," Rafe replied. "You're in a lot more trouble right here, right now, unless I get some answers." His arms flexed just once, and there was no doubt in anyone's mind that he meant business. That he wanted answers and didn't much care how he got them. That he was a man who'd resorted to violence before and would do so again without hesitation if it became necessary.

"Rafe—" T.J. wasn't sure what she would have said, but he silenced her with a quick glance. She swallowed and cradled her broken arm in her good one, and didn't interfere. It was, after all, what she had promised to do, she reminded herself. And besides that, she wanted very badly to hear the answer to Rafe's question herself.

He looked back at the perspiring young man. "Well?" His voice was very soft. Very deadly.

The young man muttered a curse, looked wildly at his scowling partner, then blurted, "McBain. The guy's name is McBain. That's all I know, man."

Nodding in satisfaction, Rafe turned to T.J. "Does that name mean anything to you?"

She was genuinely puzzled. "McBain?" she repeated, staring at the confessor. "*Councilman* McBain?"

He nodded reluctantly and looked down at his lap with a defeated slump to his shoulders.

She was stunned. Why on earth would Councilman McBain want her killed? She hardly even knew the man! She had never liked him, had voted against him in the last election, but that was the full extent of it. She said as much to Rafe.

"You've never met him?" he asked with a frown.

"I didn't say that. I've met him. Once. Briefly. He was furious that day, but not at me. At his wife. I was interviewing her and we interrupted—" She stopped suddenly, her right hand going to her mouth.

Rafe tilted his head and looked puzzled. "He wouldn't want you dead because you'd seen him yell at his wife."

"No . . ." T.J. agreed, trying hard to remember the face of the other man who'd been in that den when she and Judy McBain had walked into the room. "Oh, damn!" she said suddenly, then turned without another word and rushed out of the office.

Rafe stared at the spot where T.J. had stood, then glanced at his guards. "Keep an eye on them for me," he said as he headed toward the door. They nodded. He left without doubt that his instructions would be followed.

He found T.J. in her room, studying the newspaper that had been lying on her desk all week. She looked up when he entered the room and pointed to a photograph on the front page. "This man—"

He glanced at the photograph without recognition. "What about him?"

"His name is Ferrell Reimer, an alleged criminal with strong ties to organized crime in Atlanta. According to this article, he disappeared the same day I interviewed Judy McBain. His body was found last Sunday with a bullet through the head."

Rafe tensed. "How does this concern you?"

She set the paper back on the desk, looking at Rafe with wide, troubled eyes. "I'm almost positive that Ferrell Reimer is the man who was with Councilman McBain when Mrs. McBain and I blundered into their very private meeting. I'd never seen Reimer before, so I didn't recognize him, though I wondered why McBain was so furious that we'd interrupted them. I thought maybe he always treated his wife like dirt. Now I think maybe he was furious—and scared—because I'd seen him meeting with Reimer."

"A city councilman would certainly not want to be caught by a reporter in a meeting with a crime boss,"

Rafe agreed thoughtfully, his mind leaping a step ahead. "Especially if—"

"Especially if he had something to do with that crime boss's murder," T.J. finished for him. "As far as I know, McBain's never been connected with organized crime, though he has lots of powerful ties in the business community. It's been rumored for years that he had his eye on a Senate seat, maybe the governor's office."

"He wouldn't be the first aspiring politician to get mixed up in dangerous power games," Rafe murmured, glancing again at the folded newspaper. "Even a hint of a connection to organized crime could put any political aspirations he might have had in serious jeopardy. A definite correlation to a murdered crime boss would bring it all to a screeching halt."

"And I was so wrapped up in my problems with management and so resentful of being banished to the society pages that I totally overlooked the biggest story opportunity of my entire career," T.J. grumbled in self-disgust. "Damn, I've been an idiot! Why didn't I make this connection before?"

"Having someone trying to kill you, and damn near succeeding, is enough to interfere with anyone's deductive reasoning," Rafe assured her dryly. "The first attempts were so inept—and now that I've seen the screwups McBain hired, I understand why—that it was no wonder you wrote them off as accidents until the bomb removed all doubt that you were being targeted."

But T.J. refused to be mollified. Restlessly pacing the bedroom, she muttered, "If only I'd stopped to think about it, particularly after I saw Reimer's photograph and realized that he looked familiar. But by then I was so wrapped up in—" She stopped, as though realizing she was close to saying something indiscreet.

Rafe wondered what she'd started to say. Had it had something to do with him? He found himself reluctant to ask. Instead he returned to the more pressing subject. "You may well have been the last person— other than McBain—to see Reimer alive."

She turned to look at him. "You really think it's possible McBain killed him?"

"More than possible, I'd say. If he was this anxious to get rid of the one witness, other than his wife, who could place him and Reimer together, there has to be one hell of a reason. And since he's gone to the trouble of tracking you down and making an attempt to get at you here, he's obviously getting desperate. I'll call Atlanta, talk to the detective in charge of your case."

She nodded, her expression thoughtful. "Yes. You do that."

He lifted his head at a sound from outside. "Sounds like the police have arrived to relieve us of our prisoners. Why don't you get some rest while I take care of all this."

"No," she said, stepping toward him. "I couldn't sleep now, anyway. I'll come with you."

He wasn't particularly surprised. He put his arm around her waist as they left the suite. He had the nagging feeling that there was something he wanted to say to her, something that needed to be said now, before it was too late. But he didn't know what it was. So, he said nothing.

As they walked back into the office where his guards had been joined by several more uniformed men, he was aware of a fleeting sensation that an important opportunity had just been lost, and that he would have reason to regret it later.

He shook the feeling off and gave his full attention to the tasks at hand.

11

IT WAS LATE the next afternoon when they received word from Atlanta. McBain had been arrested and evidence had been found to indicate that he'd been blackmailed by Reimer for money and political favors because of some shady business deals several years earlier. T.J.'s testimony would tie McBain to Reimer, as well as provide evidence that he was one of the last people to see Reimer alive.

"Hiring those two men to kill you was the final knot in McBain's noose," Rafe said, summing up the telephone call he'd just received from Tristan. "Not only was the guy crooked, he was also one stupidly incompetent criminal."

T.J. nodded. "Then it's over," she said, letting the thought sink in slowly.

"Yeah. It's all over."

She wondered why she didn't feel more relief. Shouldn't she feel as though a tremendous load had just been lifted from her shoulders? But instead, she found herself nagged by a vague sense of dread, haunted by a faint mental echo...

It's over. It's all over.

"I suppose it's safe for me to go now." She looked down as she spoke, at her fingers worrying that bit of gauze on her cast.

"Anytime you like," Rafe agreed evenly.

She moistened her lips. "I guess it had better be pretty soon. I have a lot to do—a job interview to arrange—and I'm sure my family will want to see me soon. Just to see for themselves that I'm okay."

"I'm sure they will. I'll handle the arrangements for you whenever you want to go home."

Home? Couldn't he understand that she didn't even know where that was anymore? An apartment in Atlanta, a new place in South Carolina, perhaps, even her parents' house in Florida. None of them felt like home, because Rafe wouldn't be there. Because she'd be alone wherever she ended up, while the man she loved went on with his orderly life on his beautiful island.

"Maybe I'd better leave tomorrow." *Ask me not to go, Rafe. Please. Ask me to stay.*

"I'll have Jeanette make your reservations." If he had any objections to her leaving, he didn't allow it to show in his voice, or in his expressionless face.

Something twisted inside her. Since the two would-be assassins had been captured during the night, Rafe had withdrawn so far from her that she couldn't seem to reach him no matter how hard she'd tried. The only thing left for her to do was to pull back, as well, so she could leave with her dignity at least.

"By the way," he said, shoving his hands into his slacks—he was wearing white again—and resting one hip against his desk, "I have a lot of paperwork to do this afternoon, end-of-the-month stuff that usually takes several hours to complete. I'll probably have to work late. Feel free to call room service for dinner if you like, or use either of my tables if you'd rather eat out."

"Fine," she said, turning away. "I'll go do some packing now and let you get started."

"I'll send someone to help you."

"No," she said, without turning around. "Thank you, Rafe, but you've done quite enough."

She walked out of his office with her chin high, her eyes dry —and her heart in broken, bleeding shards.

RAFE STARED without moving at the empty doorway of his office long after T.J. walked out. And then he erupted in a sudden burst of fury, slashing his hand across his desk, recklessly, heedlessly, scattering the formerly neat stack of paperwork that had been waiting for his attention. A heavy brass paperweight crashed to the floor, a pencil cup fell to its side, pencils and pens tumbling out of it.

He scrubbed his hands over his face, calling himself every kind of an idiot for letting her walk away. Knowing he wouldn't try to stop her when she left for good. He had nothing to offer her if she stayed.

It was a long time before he finally released a deep, weary breath and began to return his desk to some semblance of order.

T.J. WAS SPENDING a long, miserable, sleepless night. She tossed restlessly in the big, lonely bed, longing for the escape of sleep, knowing she wouldn't be granted that release. Not tonight. Not when she'd be leaving the only man she'd ever loved in only a few short hours.

As he'd warned her, he'd worked late, or at least, he'd stayed late in his office, either working or deliberately avoiding her.

She'd finally given up and turned in, though she'd known even then she wouldn't be able to rest comfortably. She'd heard Rafe come in an hour or so later, had held her breath as his footsteps had approached her door, then had fought tears when he'd turned away. Moments later, she'd heard the door to his own room closing. It was the first time since she'd arrived that he'd closed his door to her.

For just a moment, the old, fiery, temperamental T.J. had threatened to resurface. She'd actually thrown back the bedcovers and sat up, fully intending to hammer on that closed door and demand to know why the *hell* he was suddenly treating her as though she had some sort of communicable disease! Maybe she'd even punch him right in the mouth for hurting her like this—*no one* hurt T. J. Harris without receiving full measure in return!

But then the new T.J.—the one made vulnerable by love, the one who couldn't bear to face being hurt even more cruelly by him—had taken over. She'd slid slowly back down into the pillows, knowing there was nothing she could do to make Rafe love her, no matter how badly she wanted to try.

She closed her burning eyes, turned her face into the pillow and wished she could go back to being the way she'd been before Rafe had entered her life and claimed her formerly invincible heart.

She didn't hear Rafe enter the room, and his touch on her shoulder made her open her eyes with a gasp. She stared at him, noting that he wore only a pair of denim shorts, the waistband unsnapped. Even in her misery, she couldn't help admiring the perfection of his lean, strong body; his sleek, tanned chest; flat, taut stomach; long, muscle-roped legs. His dark hair was tousled, as though he, too, had been trying unsuccessfully to sleep. She wanted him so badly she trembled with the need. "What is it, Rafe?"

"I miss having you in my bed," he answered simply, his voice a growl in the darkened, quiet room.

She swallowed, suddenly filled with nervous hope. "Do you?"

"Yes." He touched her hair, his fingers lingering at her nape. "I suppose I'll have to get used to it after you leave tomorrow."

Hope died with a silent, anguished whimper. It was all she could do to answer him evenly. "I suppose you will."

He knelt beside the bed, his dark eyes burning through the darkness. "T.J.—"

"Yes?"

He started to say something, then hesitated. When he spoke, she sensed that they weren't the words he'd originally intended.

"We have one more night. Must we spend that night alone?"

She could have sent him away, *would* have sent him away if she'd thought he was only using her, only amusing himself with her for one more night. He might have stolen her heart, but she still had her pride.

But something in his voice, something in his expression, made her hesitate. An unfamiliar diffidence? Just a hint of her own vulnerability? An undertone of that old, haunting pain that she'd always sensed in him, but had never been able to fully understand? "Rafe, I—"

His mouth was only inches from hers. "One more night, T.J. Please."

It wasn't a word that would have come easily to him. It wasn't a word she could resist from him. She lifted her mouth to his. "Come to bed, Rafe."

He groaned his approval of her decision and crushed her mouth beneath his.

Their loving was silent, frantic, almost savage. T.J. felt limp, satiated, somewhat bruised and thoroughly bewildered when it was over and Rafe slept heavily beside her.

How could he make love to her that way and not feel as strongly as she did? she asked herself again and again.

And if he was really so reluctant to see her leave, why did he seem so anxious for her to go?

THE HELICOPTER MADE a shrill, eardrum-threatening noise as it warmed up. Its blades whipped the air into a strong wind that tossed T.J.'s bangs and blew Rafe's dark hair around his stern face. Her bags had already been loaded, and the pilot was ready to take off the moment she stepped inside. She'd said her rather emotional goodbyes to Joe and Jeanette and the other members of Rafe's staff who'd befriended her. Now she had only to say goodbye to Rafe.

"I don't know how to thank you for everything you've done for me," she told him, her voice raised over the sound of the helicopter.

"You've thanked me several times," he reminded her. He glanced at the cast cradled again in the canvas sling. "Be careful with that arm."

"Yes, I will." Though she'd never seen Rafe's expression less revealing than it was now, she couldn't look away from him, couldn't seem to find the initiative to turn and board the helicopter.

She didn't want to go.

Rafe gave her a faint smile—only a shadow of his usual charming grin. "I hate goodbyes."

She nodded. "So do I."

He stepped forward, took her face between his hands and dropped a light, brief kiss on her lips. "Take care of yourself, T.J. Stay out of trouble."

She managed a smile in return. "I can't make any promises about staying out of trouble."

"No," he agreed with a slight deepening of the corners of his mouth. "Trouble seems to have a way of finding you, doesn't it?"

She looked at him steadily. "Yes. Apparently it does."

He kissed her again, longer and harder this time. And then he released her and stepped back. "Goodbye, T.J."

"Goodbye, Rafe." She wouldn't cry, she told herself firmly. She *would not* cry. Not yet, anyway.

She turned and moved toward the helicopter, her bangs whipping around her forehead, her loose-fitting shirt and pants molding themselves to her body. She'd taken only a few steps, when something made her stop and look back at him. She hardly recognized her own voice when she said, "I'd have stayed, you know. If you'd asked, I'd have stayed."

He stiffened and a muscle twitched in his jaw. Finally, he answered. "Maybe you would have stayed—for a while. Until you realized there was nothing here for you. It's better for you to go now."

She looked at him, standing there so distant and hard, and suddenly the old temper kicked in. How *dared* he tell her what she wanted, what she needed?

How did he have the gall to imply that she wasn't capable of making her own decisions?

"You blind, arrogant fool," she said, making sure the words carried clearly over the noise of the helicopter behind her. "We make our own choices, and you've obviously chosen to be a lonely martyr here on your pretty little island. Well, enjoy it. After all, you do it so very damned well."

With that she turned and ran toward the waiting helicopter. And this time she didn't look back until she was in the air, hovering above him. He was exactly where she'd left him, unmoving, his white clothing gleaming in the bright sunlight.

Why did she have the strange sensation that a dark, dreary shadow had fallen over him as he stood there alone, watching her leave?

AFTER A BRIEF VISIT with her solicitous family in Florida, T.J. returned to Atlanta, to find herself a minor celebrity, the reporter who'd survived several attempts on her life and had been responsible for unraveling one of the most controversial local murder cases in some time. Even her position with the newspaper had been considerably elevated during her absence. It seemed that being the subject of a hot story made her much more popular with her employers. Her editor offered her a political assignment she'd have fought for before. She *could* still work with a broken arm, couldn't she? he'd asked solicitously.

She'd refused to cut her sick leave short, and she planned to use that time to set up an interview with the publisher in South Carolina. She had no intention of staying with the Atlanta editors, despite the attention she was receiving from them now.

She also needed the time to get her life back in order. She lacked enthusiasm for anything—her work, her friends, her former pursuits, but she refused to let one disappointing love affair ruin her life. She'd never done so before, had she? She'd always picked herself up, dusted herself off and put it all behind her, right?

But she knew, even as she made her bracing little pep talk to her reflection in the mirror, that this time was different. This time, for the first time, she'd fallen in love. And she couldn't stop loving just because her love hadn't been returned. Couldn't so easily put it out of her mind, no matter how hard she tried to do so.

Two weeks after her return from Serendipity, she decided she'd had enough of moping around her apartment. She'd been out very little since she'd come back, had seen Gayle a time or two, but few of her other friends. Her only contact with the outside world had been the many calls she'd received, and sometimes, she'd left the answering machine on when she wasn't in the mood to talk. Now she needed to get out, see some friends, have a few drinks and a few laughs. Anything to dull the pain—if only for a few hours.

She picked up the phone and called for a cab before she could change her mind and spend another lonely evening at home.

"Yo, T.J.!" Mitchell Drisco bellowed her name the minute she stepped into the bar, waving to get her attention.

She grinned and sauntered across the crowded room to their usual little corner table, exchanging greetings with acquaintances along the way, patiently responding to questions she'd heard all too many times now, assuring everyone she was fine. Just fine, thank you.

"Why didn't you bring a bullhorn, Drisco?" she inquired dryly as she slid into a chair across the table from him. "I think there were some people on the next block that might not have heard you yell my name."

He only grinned through his bushy beard and signaled for a waitress. "I'll buy you a beer."

She choked dramatically. "*You're* buying? What's gotten into you?"

"Gee, I don't know," he murmured, his eyes glinting. "Must be that cast. Makes you look kind of wounded and helpless."

T.J.'s cutting response should have blistered his ears. Instead he only laughed and ordered their drinks. Mitchell was well acquainted with T.J.'s temper. They'd known each other socially and professionally for several years and had been friends almost from the beginning.

Before the beers arrived, a broad-shouldered black man in a rumpled patrolman's uniform joined them at the table. "Hey, T.J. Lookin' good, kid. Glad to have you back."

"Thanks, Hal. How's it going?"

He shrugged. "Same ol' same ol'."

The waitress delivered beers, including one for Hal, who hadn't been obliged to order. Hal always ordered beer. Just one, which he would nurse for however long he stayed before heading home. It had been his routine several times a week since his wife had left him two years earlier, declaring herself unable to compete with his dedication to his job.

Feeling the tense muscles at the back of her neck slowly begin to relax, T.J. wondered why she'd stayed away so long from her friends. This is what she'd needed, she mused, glancing from Mitchell to Hal. Teasing, acceptance, affection.

For a moment, she felt a pang of loss at the realization that she'd be leaving so many good friends behind when she moved away. But then she shook the feeling off, knowing she really had no choice. She needed to make a new start, needed to find a job she could launch herself into with a semblance of her old fire and enthusiasm. Maybe then she could get over this feeling that she'd left the best part of herself on an island in the Caribbean.

"Well, hail, hail, the gang's all here," Mitchell announced loudly, looking past T.J.'s shoulder. "Pull up a chair, stranger, and remind us who you are."

Tristan hooked a hand under the back of an empty chair at a nearby table and plopped it down beside T.J. "Stifle it, Mitchell," he said in his cool, clipped British accent. He settled into the chair and turned to T.J.

"I rather hoped I'd find you here when I didn't get an answer at your place."

She cocked her head in curiosity. "You were looking for me? How come?"

He smiled and lightly touched her right hand. "I just wanted to see you. I haven't seen you since Rafe snatched you out of the hospital."

Just the sound of Rafe's name sent a sharp pain through her chest. She tried to hide it by taking a long swallow of her beer before speaking. "How are Devon and the baby?"

"Fine, thank you. You wouldn't believe how quickly Courtney is growing and changing. You'll have to come have dinner with us and see for yourself."

"I'd like that," she answered lightly, thinking maybe she'd try to do so during her final week in Atlanta, as soon as she decided when that would be.

"I talked to Rafe this morning."

She looked studiously at her mug and scrubbed at a drop of moisture on the side with one fingertip, aware that Mitchell and Hal were paying close attention to her conversation with Tristan. "Did you? How is he?"

"You haven't heard from him?"

"No." She hadn't expected to really, but still she'd found herself watching the telephone. Willing it to ring. Was that why she'd been so reluctant to leave home? Because she'd been hoping Rafe would call? What an idiot she was.

"That surprises me," Tristan commented, though T.J. had the feeling he wasn't at all surprised. That he knew full well Rafe hadn't been in touch with her. Maybe even knew why. "He seemed quite concerned with your well-being. I would have thought he'd call to check on you himself."

"No," she repeated, a bit sullenly. "He hasn't called."

Tristan leaned back in his chair, long legs stretched out in front of him. "I see."

"So did you and Rafe have a fight or what?" Mitchell asked with characteristic tactlessness.

"No, Mitchell. We didn't have a fight."

"You piss him off?"

"No," she answered quellingly. "Haven't you guys got anything else to talk about? Your *own* business, perhaps?"

Mitchell cleared his throat loudly, turned to Hal and launched into a discussion of the latest Braves statistics. Tristan leaned closer to T.J., lowering his voice so that she was the only one who could hear him. "Rafe's a good man, T.J. One of the best friends I've ever had."

"I know. But, Tristan—"

He silenced her with an upraised hand. "I just want you to know that I understand. He's got walls around him that might as well be made of concrete. I can see where a woman like you would find that difficult to live with. But he built those walls not because he cares too little, but because he has always cared too much. Can you understand that?"

She nodded slowly. "I know it has to do with his former job. Something is still eating him alive, and he can't seem to get past it and go on with his life."

"Maybe he could—with a little help from someone who loves him. Someone strong enough and stubborn enough to get through to him."

"What makes you think I love him?" T.J. demanded with just a touch of her old bravado.

His smile was gentle, affectionate and much too knowing. "Did you honestly think you could hide something like that from me, Tyler Jessica? And," he added just as she drew back her foot, "if you kick me again I'm going to turn you over my knee right here in front of everyone. I swear I will."

She set her foot back on the floor, though she met his amused eyes defiantly. "What makes you think you could?"

"I'd damned well try," he retorted. "I didn't say it would be easy. I've never known you to give up on a fight, T.J. Never thought I'd hear you admit defeat."

Her temper dissipated with a long sigh. "Don't use psychology on me, Parrish. You know that always annoys me."

"Just think about what I said, okay? I don't like seeing my friends in pain."

"I'd like to talk about something else now, Tristan. Tell me more about Courtney. Do you have any new pictures?"

She was greatly relieved when he reached for his wallet, and she knew he wouldn't say any more about Rafe.

Didn't Tristan understand that T.J. would have done anything she could to make it work with Rafe, if only Rafe had shown any sign that he was willing to meet her halfway? Should she tell him that it had been Rafe's choice, not hers, for her to leave the island?

She wouldn't tell him, of course. She was clinging too tightly to her pride.

Her pride was all that she had left.

RAFE STOOD on his bluff, overlooking the resort that had once seemed such a refuge to him. Now, everywhere he looked, he saw T.J. In his office, in the restaurants, on the beach, in his suite. In his bed.

He missed her.

He'd spent more hours brooding in this spot during the month since she'd left than he ever had before. The shadows haunted him, pressed closer and closer to him. There were times when he thought they'd swallow him whole.

Why had he let her walk away, knowing she would have stayed if he'd only asked? Why, for the first time in his life, had he let sheer cowardice rule his actions? Why hadn't he given the two of them a chance?

He thought of her living her life without him. Had she found a new job yet? Was her arm healing without complications? Was she taking care of herself?

Was she seeing anyone else?

He missed her, dammit!

He stared bleakly at the shadow-dulled landscape spread out beneath him and called himself a fool.

T.J. FLEXED her arms, clenching and unclenching her fists, noted without a great deal of interest that her left arm still looked pale and thin in comparison to her right. The cast had been removed the day before and she'd been assured the arm would be back to normal before long. She hoped so. It would be nice to know that something about her was back to normal.

She looked at the computer screen in front of her and tried to concentrate on the article she was writing to be faxed to the editor in South Carolina. They'd been talking and corresponding for a couple of weeks, and he was definitely interested in her work, though T.J. hadn't yet committed to a date when she'd be available to work full-time for him. She poised her hands above the keyboard, typed a sentence, read it twice, deleted it. And then her hands fell back into her lap.

The telephone at her elbow rang. She picked it up without much enthusiasm. She didn't know who had dialed her number—it was enough that she knew who *wasn't* calling.

It was Gayle, who tried to talk T.J. into going shopping or to a movie. "We haven't spent a day together in weeks," she added wistfully.

"Thanks, Gayle, but I really can't today. I need to work."

Gayle sighed deeply, sounding discouraged. "All right. I understand. But T.J., you'll call if you need me?"

"Of course I will," T.J. promised, knowing her friend worried about her, that all her friends were worried about her. She despised herself for acting like a lovesick adolescent.

She was aware of a nagging headache when she hung up. She wandered into the bathroom for acetaminophen tablets. "What are you going to do?" she demanded aloud of the woeful reflection in the mirror over the sink. "Spend the rest of your life moping over this man? Grow up, Harris. Get a life!"

Maybe it was the sight of that dejected-looking face staring back at her from the mirror. Or maybe she was just tired of being miserable. Suddenly T.J. knew that enough was enough. It was time to get on with her life, with or without Rafe.

"You're a wimp, Harris," she said slowly as she stared into that mirror.

All her life she'd been willing to fight for what she'd wanted, yet she'd walked away from the only man she'd ever loved—the only man she *would* ever love—without a protest. What had happened to her spirit? Her guts? Her determination?

Was she going to let love turn her into a whining loser? Or was she going to do something about this mess?

Rafe loved her, dammit. He had to. The way he'd made love to her, the way he'd fought to protect her, the look in his eyes when they'd said goodbye—whether he knew it or not, he loved her. And she hadn't even tried to make him admit it.

She marched out of the bathroom and headed straight for the telephone on her desk. She was going to call her travel agent and make arrangements for another trip to Serendipity. It would clean out her savings, but this time she intended to find out once and for all if there was any chance that she and Rafe could build a lasting relationship.

If he could look her in the eye and tell her he didn't care, that he didn't want to try, fine. She'd survive. She might even punch him in the stomach while she was at it for putting her through all this in the first place.

At least she'd know she'd made an effort. At least she wouldn't have to keep agonizing over whether there was something else she should have said, something she should have done. . . .

She'd just entered the first three digits of her travel agent's telephone number, when her doorbell rang. She thought about ignoring it, then slammed her phone down when the bell buzzed again, sounding more impatient this time. It was probably another one of her friends, checking on her. She wouldn't encourage whoever it was to stay for long. She had plans to make. A stubborn, thick-skulled male to confront.

She snatched open the door without checking to see who waited outside. And then realized in stunned pleasure that she wouldn't have to chase Rafe, after all. He had come to her, looking infinitely appealing and subtly dangerous in a black T-shirt and worn jeans.

Without even stopping to think about it, she doubled her fist and punched him in the stomach.

12

RAFE WAS CAUGHT off guard. His breath escaped in a surprised whoosh as he doubled into the blow. And then he grinned and stepped into T.J.'s apartment, kicking the door closed behind him with one booted foot.

She backed up warily, but didn't look particularly afraid of what he'd do in retaliation. T.J. was the one woman who'd never shown any fear of him, not even when he'd demonstrated quite graphically how violent he could be if necessary. That fiery spirit of hers had attracted him from the beginning. "Nice to see you, too, honey."

"Don't call me 'honey,'" she responded automatically. "What are you doing here, Rafe?"

"I had a taste of martyrdom, and I didn't care for it," he replied. "I'm tired of being alone on my pretty little island, T.J. Tired of my own depressing company."

"Have you thought about getting a dog?" she suggested coolly, her arms crossed nonchalantly over her chest.

He might have been discouraged by her apparent indifference to his words if he hadn't seen the joy that had flashed in her eyes a moment before she'd punched him. "I don't want a dog," he murmured with a smile. "I want you."

"Sorry. I'd make a lousy pet. I'd be a total washout in obedience training, for one thing. And I'd never be content to sit around chasing my own tail while you went off to brood on your private bluff," she added. "Waiting for you to come back and pat me on the head and send me to my corner when I started demanding too much from you. Like honesty. And respect. And trust."

"I know I hurt you. But I—"

"*Hurt me?*" she repeated, her words slicing into his explanation. "You didn't just hurt me, Rafe. You damned near destroyed me. And I tried very hard to hate you for that."

He cupped her face in his hands and looked down at her with his heart in his eyes. "Did you succeed?" he murmured, sliding one thumb across her full lower lip. "*Do* you hate me, T.J.?"

Her hands slid up his chest. "No," she whispered, her eyes darkening as she tilted her mouth upward. "No, damn you. I—"

He kissed her before she could say anything else, unable to wait another moment to taste her again. It seemed like forever since the last time he'd kissed her.

T.J.'s mouth opened to his with an eagerness that belied her initial show of indifference. He kissed her until he was almost dizzy from lack of oxygen, raised his head only to take a deep breath and then kissed her again. He moved his hands feverishly over her body, reacquainting himself with the feel of her. Was she thinner now than she'd been before?

His arms tightened around her. "God, how I've missed you," he said thickly, his mouth still hovering over her moist, slightly swollen lips.

She hugged him closer. "I've missed you, too, Rafe."

Suddenly aware of just how tightly she was holding him, he held her a few inches away and looked at her left arm with a smile of delight. "The cast is gone."

"Yesterday."

"Congratulations."

"Thanks. Do you want a drink or something?" she asked, as though suddenly aware of her duties as a hostess.

Rafe grinned at her sudden solicitousness. This was the woman he loved, he thought contentedly. Punching him in the stomach one minute, offering him a drink the next. He wouldn't have changed a thing about her. T.J. would never bore him. "I don't want a drink right now, but I would like to sit down. We need to talk. Might as well get comfortable."

Her smile dimmed, as though she wasn't quite sure she'd like what he had to say. He gave her a reassuring smile and led her to the couch. He sat at one end and pulled her down close beside him.

"You said you wanted honesty," he began after clearing his throat. "Respect. Trust."

"Yes. I can deal with your moods, Rafe, but I can't live with the walls you put between us," she said, looking at him rather anxiously. "I need to know what drives you, what haunts you. Why you feel as though you have to hold yourself apart at times from everyone else, including me?"

He took a deep breath and started talking, telling her things he'd never told anyone else. Not even Tristan, who knew most, but not all of Rafe's story. He told her how the dangerous, adventurous side of his former undercover career had drawn him in, pulling him deeper and deeper into a life that most people could never imagine. About the dark, ugly side of his work. How the danger and intrigue had grown more distasteful with every passing year.

He explained how the lines between the good guys and the bad guys had begun to blur, then to overlap. How many innocents had been swept into the drug war he'd fought—the ten-year-old boy who'd been killed when Rafe's cover had been blown on his last assignment.

"Manuel," T.J. said, holding his hands tightly in her own, as she had since he'd started speaking.

Startled, he stared at her. "How did you—oh. The nightmares."

"Yes. You called his name in your sleep. You always sounded so sad, so tormented. It broke my heart."

"I blamed myself," Rafe admitted in a low voice. "He was just a kid, dammit. Just a kid. Everyone tried to tell me it wasn't my fault, that there was nothing I could have done to save him, but I still blamed myself. If only—" He broke off with a weary sigh and shook his head. "Too many 'if onlys.' For the past four years I've been haunted by his face and a dozen others—friends, enemies, innocent bystanders. Too many faces—too many victims."

"You learned to lock your feelings away," T.J. said, her eyes wide with comprehension. "You couldn't have done your job and retained your sanity if you hadn't. And because you'd lost your family so devastatingly, you learned to guard your emotions, not to get too close. Even to your wife."

He nodded. "I could lock my feelings away—most of the time. Not always."

"No. You're a man who cares too much, Rafe. You weren't able to go on pretending differently for long. Your guilt and your grief tormented you—in your sleep, during your down times, your 'moods.'"

"Like shadows blocking the sun," he murmured.

"You need to talk about your feelings, not push them aside and try to deny them," she said earnestly, her hands clasped warmly around his. "You have to get your troubles out in the open if you're going to overcome them. You can't fight something you can't see or won't acknowledge."

"I've gotten most of it out in the open today," he admitted. "I've told you more than I've ever told anyone before."

"How does it feel?"

He thought about it a moment, surprised to find that the load *had* lightened, at least a little. That he could live with his past as long as he knew there was hope for a brighter future.

A future with T.J.

"It feels pretty good," he said.

She smiled. "I'm glad."

"I love you, T.J."

Her hands went slack in his. He held his breath as he waited for her to respond. He wasn't sure if she'd kiss him and tell him she loved him, too, or whether she'd slug him again.

T.J. was never predictable.

"You're—um—practicing sharing your feelings again, I take it?" she asked somewhat shakily.

"Yeah. How am I doing?"

"Showing real potential."

He began to relax. "Then I might as well go all the way with it. I love you. I want to marry you. I want to have kids with you and grow old with you. I want to spend the rest of my life with you. What do you say?"

"I—" She closed her mouth, swallowed hard, then shook her head slowly, looking utterly dazed. "I don't know *what* to say."

"You've gotta learn to share your feelings, honey," he advised her with a smile that he hoped hid the extent of his anxiety. "You might want to start by telling me how you feel about me...."

She looked down at their hands. "I—uh—well, I—"

"Don't be such a coward, T.J. Spit it out."

She glared at him. "All right, I love you. Are you happy now?"

He could have shouted with joy. Instead he forced himself to nod coolly, as though her answer had been nothing more than he'd expected. "And?"

"And okay, I'll marry you. But I warn you, I'll probably make your life miserable. I'll be a terrible wife. I don't know how to cook—"

"I have two gourmet chefs and a half-dozen assistant chefs on my payroll. You don't have to cook."

"I'm a rotten housekeeper—"

"Maid service, remember?"

"I'm lousy at compromising. And I really hate to lose an argument."

"We'll both learn to compromise. And you'll get used to losing arguments," he said smugly.

"Don't bet on it," she retorted.

He only smiled. "Anything else I should be prepared for?"

"About that having kids business—"

"Yes?"

"I'd probably be a disaster as a mother. I don't know the first thing about babies."

"You'll be a wonderful mother. And I'll be there to help you with them. Always."

"Then I guess we've covered everything," she said a bit weakly, blinking as though she were still trying to believe she'd just gotten herself engaged.

His smile faded. "Not quite everything."

"What?"

"Your job."

"Oh."

"I know how important your career is to you, T.J., and I understand you can't pursue it on Serendipity," he began earnestly. "That's one of the reasons I hesitated to ask you to stay—that and my own stupidity," he added wryly.

"I had already decided to quit the job here," she reminded him.

"Yes, but you had plans to find another one in your profession," he said, fretting. "I don't want to hold you back, T.J. You're too good to let your talent go to waste. What I'm trying to say is that we don't have to live on the island. I can hire managers for the resorts, run the business from somewhere else, plan regular visits to supervise and double-check the operations. As soon as you find a job you like, we'll start making plans to settle there."

She had to clear her throat twice before she could answer. He was surprised, and rather shaken, to see that her eyes had filled with tears. "I'm touched that you'd make an offer like that for me," she said at length, holding her voice steady with a visible effort. "It means more to me than you could possibly know."

"I'm serious."

"I know you are. But it won't be necessary. At least not for now. I know how much you love living on Serendipity."

"Not as much as I love you," he argued.

She smiled, the tears drying. "I'm offering a compromise here, Rafe. Try to be gracious about it, will you?"

He returned the smile. "What's your compromise?"

"I take some time off from working full-time to concentrate on writing a satirical political column—

for national syndication, I hope. I talk to the editor in South Carolina who's so enthused about my work and convince him that I can submit material from our home on Serendipity. All I need to get started are subscriptions to a few dozen newspapers and newsmagazines, satellite television hookups, a computer modem and a fax machine. Think that can be arranged?"

"I'll set you up with anything you need," he answered promptly, eagerly. "The best of everything— state-of-the-art communications."

She frowned slightly. "We'll call it a business loan," she said. "I'll pay back your investment when I start earning a salary."

"How about calling it a partnership, instead?" he suggested, lifting her hands to his lips.

"We'll discuss it," she agreed, catching her breath when his lips brushed her knuckles. "Later."

"Yes." He dropped her hands and reached for her, pulling her roughly into his arms. "Much later. I love you, T.J."

Her two strong, healthy arms reached up around his neck. "I love you, too."

"It won't always be easy, being married to me," he warned one last time, between nibbles at her neck. "I can't promise I won't still get moody sometimes, or that there won't still be times when my past crops up to haunt me."

"I'll be there when it does, to help you fight those shadows," she promised, arching her back to offer him more of her. "But I can't promise that I won't lose my temper sometimes, or be difficult to live with."

"We'll quarrel," he agreed, smiling in wry anticipation, his hand creeping up her side to the top button of her blouse. "And we'll make up. Spectacularly."

She sighed dreamily. "It's nice to have something to look forward to."

"In the meantime . . ." He released that top button and moved down to the next.

"Mmm." She was already tugging at the hem of his T-shirt. "In the meantime . . ."

Rafe bore her down into the cushions of the couch, knowing he had everything he wanted, everything he could ever ask for right here in his arms. T.J. was everything he'd ever wanted in a woman—strong, courageous, loyal, tempestuous. Everything he could have asked for in a mate, and a mother for the children they'd have when the time was right.

As he threw himself into the fire they ignited with their passion, he allowed himself to believe for the first time that the shadows had been banished forever.

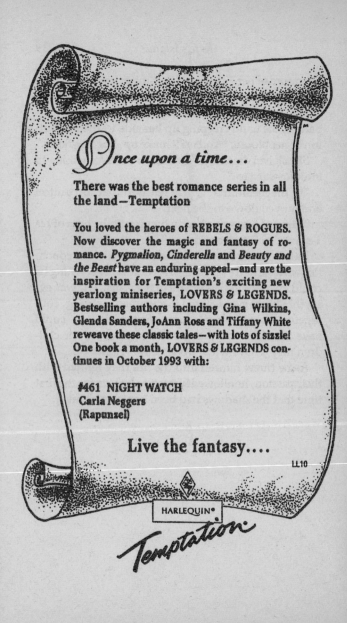

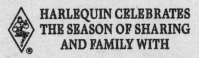

**HARLEQUIN CELEBRATES
THE SEASON OF SHARING
AND FAMILY WITH**

Friends, Families, Lovers

Harlequin introduces the latest member in its family of
seasonal collections. Following in the footsteps of the popular
My Valentine, Just Married and *Harlequin Historical Christmas
Stories*, we are proud to present FRIENDS, FAMILIES,
LOVERS. A collection of three new contemporary romance
stories about America at its best, about welcoming others into
the circle of love.... Stories to warm your heart ...

By three leading romance authors:

> **KATHLEEN EAGLE
> SANDRA KITT
> RUTH JEAN DALE**

> Available in October, wherever
> Harlequin books are sold.

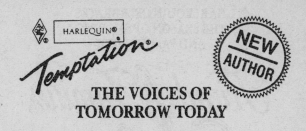

HARLEQUIN®

Temptation

NEW AUTHOR

THE VOICES OF TOMORROW TODAY

Sensuous, bold, sometimes controversial, Harlequin Temptation novels are stories of women today—the attitudes, desires, lives and language of the nineties.

The distinctive voices of our authors is the hallmark of Temptation. We are proud to announce two new voices are joining the spectacular Temptation lineup.

Kate Hoffman, *INDECENT EXPOSURE*, #456, August 1993

Jennifer Crusie, *MANHUNTING*, #463, October 1993

Tune in to the hottest station on the romance dial—Temptation!

HARLEQUIN®

Temptation®

FIRST-PERSON PERSONAL

Nothing is more intimate than first-person personal
narration....

Two emotionally intense, intimate romances told in first
person, in the tradition of Daphne du Maurier's *Rebecca* from
bestselling author Janice Kaiser.

Recently widowed Allison Stephens travels to her husband's
home to discover the truth about his death and finds herself
caught up in a web of family secrets and betrayals. Even more
dangerous is the passion ignited in her by the man her husband
hated most—Dirk Granville.
BETRAYAL, Temptation #462, October 1993

P.I. Darcy Hunter is drawn into the life of Kyle Weston, the
man who had been engaged to her deceased sister. Seeing him
again sparks long-buried feelings of love and guilt. Working
closely together on a case, their attraction escalates. But Darcy
fears it is memories of her sister that Kyle is falling in love with.
DECEPTIONS, Temptation #466, November 1993

Each book tells you the heroine's compelling story in her own
personal voice. Wherever Harlequin books are sold.

LIGHTS, CAMERA, ACTION!

Hollywood Dynasty

HARLEQUIN®
Temptation

The Kingstons are Hollywood—two generations of box-office legends in front of and behind the cameras. In this fast-paced world egos compete for the spotlight and intimate secrets make tabloid headlines. Gage—the cinematographer, Pierce—the actor and Claire—the producer struggle for success in an unpredictable business where a single film can make or break you.

By the time the credits roll, will they discover that the ultimate challenge is far more personal? Share the behind-the-scenes dreams and dramas in this blockbuster miniseries by Candace Schuler!

THE OTHER WOMAN, #451 (July 1993)
JUST ANOTHER PRETTY FACE, #459 (September 1993)
THE RIGHT DIRECTION, #467 (November 1993)

Coming soon to your favorite retail outlet.
